Night of Fire

THE ETHER CHRONICLES

Night of Fire

The Ether Chronicles

NICO ROSSO

AVONIMPULSE
An Imprint of HarperCollins*Publishers*

This is a work of fiction. Names, characters, places, and incidents are products of the author's imagination or are used fictitiously and are not to be construed as real. Any resemblance to actual events, locales, organizations, or persons, living or dead, is entirely coincidental.

EPub Edition JULY 2012 ISBN: 9780062201089

Print Edition ISBN: 9780062201096

10 9 8 7 6 5 4 3 2 1

For Ami.
Even the gears of fate couldn't keep us apart.

Chapter One

The Sierra Madre Mountains, California

HE WORE HIS gun. And hoped he wouldn't have to use it. The war was behind him. Tom Knox headed west.

His saddle creaked. The ends of the leather reins slapped lightly against the body of his steed. The wind whistled in his ears. Six hundred feet below him, smaller hills gathered into a larger mountain range.

Instead of being filled with screaming ether-charged bullets and explosive cannon shells, the sky here was peaceful. A red-tailed hawk skimmed below him, head twitching from side to side, tracking prey. In the distance, three turkey vultures spun wide circles over a shady hill. Tom was part of the calm. His Sky Charger kept a steady pace, pushed by the high whispering whir of the tetrol-powered fan at the back.

Weeks ago, the skies to the east and behind him had burned. Enemy airships and friendly Sky Trains had blazed brighter than the sun as they crashed toward the vast soya fields of the Great Plains. Men had fought and died.

As an Upland Ranger in the U.S. Army, he'd seen it all. He'd smelled the gunpowder and felt the recoil of his Gatling rifle as he fought to turn the Hapsburgs away from American soil. A couple of searing-hot bullets had found their way into his flesh, but he'd healed fast enough to get back onto his ether-borne Sky Charger and fly into war.

TOM LEANED FORWARD, patting the cool zinc metal neck of the charger. Strange modern times he was living in. When he'd left this territory three years ago, it was on a real horse.

Adjusting the levers at his stirrups, he took the charger higher into the air. Tall pines whisked beneath him, then thinned as the rocky peaks took over. White patches of snow clung to the shaded angles of the mountains like forgotten sun-bleached bones.

Just at the top of the range, Tom stopped his charger and turned to look behind him. The battlefields and scarred skies were hundreds of miles away. The fighting wasn't over. The war waited.

He stared into the distance, remembering all the Hapsburg soldiers alive and dead who'd aimed their guns at him.

Keep your pants on, he thought. *You'll have plenty of chances to put me in a grave later. Until then, I'm heading home.*

Kicking the charger's levers, he powered the one-man ether airship over the mountain ridge, leaving the flat expanse of the east at his back. The mountains spread out into hills that bunched and gathered like an unmade bed. The green foliage of winter still lasted, revealing the fertile farms and orchards that took advantage of any flat land.

Tom squinted behind his goggles and pulled the brim of his black cavalry hat low. The far horizon was a bright, silver knife's edge. The Pacific Ocean. He could already smell the salt, even this far inland. A few more miles and he'd hear the gulping squawk of the seagulls that rode the high wind currents. It felt like home.

The hairs at the back of his neck stood up, same as if he and other Upland Rangers were flying out for a dawn raid on a Hapsburg artillery camp. There was plenty of danger at the front lines of the war. And battles to be fought at the home front.

The Sky Charger picked up speed. Tom felt himself pulled into the inevitable.

He reined back on the mechanical steed and wound over the hills. Twisted oaks dotted the land. Through the lenses of his goggles, they almost looked like their branches were outstretched arms, warning him. But there was no turning back.

The war had stopped to take a breath. Tom and other front-line soldiers were allowed some time of their own.

Without a fight in front of him, his compass spun. There was no answer other than west. Home to Thornville.

And Rosa.

A needling voice in his head sounded a lot like his younger self, mean with an edge of whiskey on his breath. *Surely seeing her again will go as smooth as silk*. It mocked him.

He tugged at the knot of the black bandana around his neck. The charger dipped closer to the ground, heading toward a shady notch running between the hills. The mechanical flying horse didn't shiver or twitch its muscles in response to coming closer to home.

Tom took a long breath and spoke in a whisper, quickly lost to the breeze. "Nothing was ever easy with Rosa."

Don't lie. Looking at Rosa had been easy. Before he'd left town three years ago, he could sit and stare at her until all the candles burned down in his one-room shack. There seemed to be no end to the depths of her large, dark brown eyes. Black hair framed her face, high cheekbones and full mouth. Tom had memorized every detail. He didn't need to carry a small lumiscopic picture of his sweetheart like other soldiers did.

But she wasn't his sweetheart anymore. A stolen horse and a moonless ride out of town had made sure of that.

Maybe a raid on a Hapsburg camp would be easier than going home after all.

The sound of the charger's tetrol engine was quickly drowned out by the loud roar of a rushing river. It tumbled along a winding path and Tom followed it, trading the steady sun for shade. Where the river widened and calmed, he took the charger even lower toward the water.

If the mechanical horse had had legs, it would've been standing chest deep in the water. Tom tipped his hat back, letting it rest against his shoulders by the stampede strap. He pulled off his goggles and clipped them to the leather lanyard slung over his shoulder. The other end of this lanyard was looped through the butt of the pistol on his hip. He didn't need to look to know it was still there after the long flight over the planes. The weight of the Rattler was a steady presence.

Leaning low over the side of the charger, Tom dipped his bandana in the cool river water. The silk danced in the flow, tugged with the current, pulled toward Thornville and Rosa. He drew the bandana from the river and used the cool cloth to wipe the dust from his face. After tying it around his neck, he went back to the water, filling his canteen, taking a long drink and filling the canteen again. Mountain water tasted of cool stone, pure and fresh. A relief after the muddy streams of the Great Plains.

He unbuckled the auxiliary reservoir from one of the saddlebags. The Sky Charger wasn't a real horse, but he still had to water it. He filled the tin tank with water and then screwed on the top.

Everything was squared away. Tom could keep moving. But he stayed, hovering over the running water.

That voice kept stabbing at him. *Rosa's down at the river. Doing the wash, or collecting water. Probably gathering blackberries. Safe and secure, like her parents wanted for her. Not like anything you could've given her. No land, no family. Just a wildcat breaking horses for hourly pay.*

Tom tried to swat the voice away as if it were a night mosquito, but it went on. *Bet she took Parker's offer and married him. That guy was a great carpenter.* The dull brass of the wedding band around Tom's finger seemed almost black in the shadows over the river.

He kicked the Sky Charger's ascend lever and climbed higher into the sky. Parker built nice things. Cabinets and tables and a stable life. His tools were handed down from his father and his father's father. All Tom had of his family was a dead-end last name and the saddle he sat on.

The voice in his head was silent, but present, mocking him.. Tom responded to himself, *I'm gonna play it as cool as snowmelt when I see her.*

Horseshit. His younger self spat and took a drink from a cloudy bottle.

Tom countered, *I can be a gentleman and tip my hat and congratulate her on her marriage.*

But when he'd see her parents, that would be another story. Tom shifted his weight in the saddle, feeling the Rattler on his hip, the Gatling rifle in the scabbard at his knee and the knife in his boot. Might need every bit of hardware to get out of a "conversation" with Rosa's mother and father.

After the din of the front lines and the skies raining fire all around, all he wanted was a little peace and quiet. But if that were true, he'd find another mountain range or another town, where no one knew his name. He had to go to Thornville. Even if there was no one waiting for him, no yellow ribbons, no family. He'd just drunk his fill of river water, but thinking about Rosa made him thirsty all over again.

"Peace and quiet." He said it out loud as if that could make it real. "How hard can that be to find?"

The river bent and dove into a jumble of rocks. Tom pulled on his hat and flew higher, breaking from the trees and nearly running straight into the side of a three-story mobile mining machine.

He yanked hard on the reins, wheeling in the air to avoid the wooden slats that made up the outer structure. A blast of invisible heat washed over him as he passed an exhaust stack from one of the tetrol engines that powered the lumbering beast. All of the cool calm he'd pulled from the river burned away.

"What in holy hellfire . . . ?"

Turning the charger again, he dove toward one of the several men who walked next to the giant machine. Tom had to shout over the sound of the giant conveyor treads that propelled the beast forward.

"You boys got a lot of nerve breaking up the scenery out here."

The man tensed slightly, revealing a black rotary shotgun slung over his shoulder and an ether pistol in a holster. A lot of hardware for a dude in a pinstripe suit. Tom's Rattler was ready at his hip if he needed it.

But hopefully, words would be enough and he could leave the shooting to the war. "What claim you headed to?"

No response from the man. He only turned and looked at Tom. It was almost like a piece of the mining machine had broken off and walked like a human being. The man wore a leather and brass mask that encased him from his bowler hat to his jaw. A shiny brass capsule covered the man's mouth and a flexible metal tube ran from the mask to a cup attached to his ear.

"Goddamn." Tom had seen this technology before on guards stationed around a bank in Chicago. "Whisperers."

The din of the rolling mining machine swallowed the man's low words, but Tom could tell he was saying something by the way he moved. The communication was broadcast out to the others around the device and they all turned to look at Tom. Sunlight glared off the glass goggles built into the masks. There were at least twenty Whisperers, all armed and coordinated by their masks.

Even though everyone knew there was over a million dollars' worth of gold locked in that Chicago bank, no one dared take on the Whisperers to try and nab it. It was like facing a single man who had forty eyes looking in every direction and guns at the ready.

"I get that you won't tell me your claim, but there's got to be a gang boss around here who can talk."

The men just kept watching him as the machine rolled forward. It was still folded up for travel, but when it reached its destination its teeth would be deployed to eat through anything in its way. Giant saws, grinding wheels, and conveyer belts would stick out of the front, tearing apart a mountainside and drawing it inside the device. Then automated sifting trays would shake the debris, searching for gold or silver or whatever the mining company decided was valuable that day.

"We all got a job to do." Tom's patience was shrinking, crushed under the treads of the mining machine. "But you're dealing with a sergeant in the U.S. Army Upland Rangers. I'm asking you a question and you're obliged to answer me."

The man moved and Tom nearly drew his Rattler. The first bullet would hit the Whisperer in the chest, if things came to that. But Tom's reflexes were good enough to hold off shooting the man. The pin-striped man wasn't going for his gun, he was merely pointing at a spot on the mining machine.

A brass plaque riveted to the side of the rolling monster read: MODEL IV. CRANDALL MINING COMPANY. SAN BERNARDINO, CALIFORNIA.

"All right then, it's someone else's problem." He kicked a lever on his charger, rising higher in the air. "Just wish your machine was as quiet as you dudes."

The technological din was left behind. Tom was back in the quiet and calm of the sky. *That's right,* he told himself. *Let everyone else deal with the world's problems.* He'd been fighting fiercely for months and it felt like the United States had been holding its breath trying to resist the Hapsburg advance. Now was the time for a sigh of relief. Some brave sons of bitches had snuck deep into the enemy's homeland and blown up a key munitions plant.

Those shock waves carried all the way to the Great Plains. One minute Tom was running belt after belt of ammo through his shoulder Gatling rifle, trying to pick off flying skiffs full of Hapsburg shock troops; the next minute the bad guys were circling their airships way behind their lines and trying to figure out what to do next.

"I know what I'm doing next." He licked his lips as the landscape rolled far below him. Saying it out loud might make it real. "Chicken. Berry pie. A shade tree . . ." That was how he and Rosa would spend long summer days at a hidden spot at the bank of the river. Her kisses were always sweeter than any berry they found in the brambles.

Goddamn, it might be the worst idea to come back. He didn't want to see her. A new life, married and happy and safe and secure with someone else. He had to see her, even if she hated him. There was only one bit of pleasure he'd known in this world and it was Rosa. The rest was hardship. His thirst returned. But being close to Rosa again without having her might be like drinking fire.

Tom had never seen this country from these heights. This was the territory he'd grown up in, but the land seemed so different: like a dream, knowing it's right, but feeling something was wrong. He was lost, but knew where he was headed.

Keeping the distant shining ocean to his left, Tom rode north. The river flickered below him, a snake hidden in shadows. He crested a hill, then another. Homesteads appeared in the flats. And in a far clearing at the base of a tall mountain he saw Thornville.

Three years had pushed the town further into where the trees had stood. What had been one wide road was now two, a cross of buildings with boardwalks and even a clock tower. Houses were scattered around the town.

There was more to this area than just farming and canning blackberries now. Maybe one of those houses was Rosa's.

His mouth went dry. She was close. There were people out on the street, but he couldn't identify them or know what they were up to from this distance. Could she see him high in the air?

Tom had left Thornville by riding away on the dusty trails. He returned in the air, a different man. But would Rosa know that?

He'd snuck out of town on a stolen horse. Coming back straight down the main street wasn't right. Tom curled a wide arc around the approaching town, putting the silver sea to his back. The pines and scrub oak were still thick enough on the other side of the river to give him a nice private place to land.

He brought the charger down, leaves brushing against his thighs, and took the metal head right next to a thick tree. While the hovering craft was still four feet off the ground, he dismounted. The ground under his feet didn't feel stable after all that time in the saddle. He took a few steps to loosen up, then pulled on the side lever of the charger, bringing it to the ground.

"Rest easy, girl. You deserve it." He locked the Gatling rifle in its scabbard, then lifted the metal covering at the charger's flank, exposing some of the inner workings. One flip of a switch and the tetrol engine stopped chugging. Tom reached deeper inside the body, to where the ether tanks glowed green through their glass ends. "Wish I could give you an apple." Instead he yanked on the pins next to the ether tanks' valves and slipped them into his shirt pocket.

The tanks stopped catalyzing ether and the charger rested completely on the dirt. Tom gave it one last pat on the side. Dry oak leaves crunched under his boots as he walked toward town. The smell of their dust took him back to being a boy, running through this land, trying to find tarantulas or deer bones. Not long after that, he was sneaking around these parts searching for Rosa.

Tom pulled a plump blackberry from a thicket next to the river. It was sweet and only reminded him of her. The plant's thorns barely scratched his toughened skin. Could he avoid Rosa's thorns?

The old bridge with some new wood still spanned the narrow part of the river near town. Here it was, the last place he'd seen her. The running water tumbling over the rocks sounded like the echoes of him and Parker yelling at each other. Couldn't have been the way Parker wanted his marriage proposal to Rosa to play out. The carpenter might've been expecting some tears of joy, not her storming off while Tom and Parker bloodied their knuckles on each other. But Tom had been freshly burned by her parents and didn't take kindly to another man moving in so fast and asking for his girl's hand. And taking on Parker was a fight he knew he could win.

Tom shook off the memories and stepped closer to the river. As he crossed the bridge and got closer to town, he realized that the echoes weren't the lingering ghosts of his final clash with Parker and Rosa. The yelling was real. There was trouble in Thornville.

He picked up his pace, following the sounds of the conflict. Someone was getting punched and going down in a lot of pain. Others shouted encouragement. Tom certainly didn't want in on a brawl, but even if everyone in town had forgotten his name, Thornville was still his home.

Ducking between a candy shop and a women's dress store, Tom got his first look at the main street. Six or seven men stood in a wide ring around two fighters. One of them staggered on wobbly legs, trying to make fists. The other stood his ground, ready. Something flashed bright on his chest, making Tom blink away the bright streak. A tin star.

"Aw, hell," Tom muttered. "Just the sheriff running some drunks out of town."

The badge flashed again and Tom refocused his eyes on the sheriff.

It was Rosa.

"THIS STAR ISN'T a fashion accessory." If only Rosa had a nickel for every time some drunken jackass thought he'd challenge the law just because she was a woman. "How do you think I got to be sheriff? By rousting a bunch of drunks like you out of town. First two rules of Thornville: no guns and no fighting." The man still gathered himself to brawl while the others cheered him on. "Clear out before things get really rough."

The drunken cowboy smiled, creasing his sunburned face. "I'm a rough rider."

Rosa shook her head and pulled the leather gloves tighter against her fists. After this fight was done she'd have to give a good talking to Francis in the saloon. *He's got to know better than to keep serving hooligans once they're this pickled.*

"After I knock you in the dust," she pointed at the man in front of her while keeping her eye on the others surrounding them, "none of y'all can show your *caras feas* in this town again."

The drunk maintained his awkward grin. "Come on. Let's do it in the dust." Then he came swinging.

He was taller than her by at least six inches. And he might've had one hundred pounds on her. But he was slow and telegraphed his first punch. It was a looping right hook. She slipped under it and drove her fist into his ribs, right over the man's kidney.

The crowd winced. The man grunted and spun, trying to slap her with the back of his hand. She anticipated this and easily ducked underneath. He wasn't smiling anymore. The pain sobered him.

"Good." She kept her fists high and ready. "I want you to be awake for every second. You might learn something." She kept a mean face, but somewhere inside, she was actually enjoying this. Swagger, even in a fight. It hadn't seemed possible until she'd seen Tom do just that in Porterville, one town downriver.

The inner joy died. Tom only fought when it was easy. High stakes had driven him out of town and out of her life. Three damn years ago. Rosa didn't know when her hurt and anger would go away. At least she could take it out on the hooligan in front of her.

He swayed his big barrel chest from side to side, as if that would make him a difficult target. Before he could attack again, she faked to the left, drawing his guard that way, then sent her fist into his neck, just below his jaw. Sputtering, the man stumbled backward into the arms of two of his friends.

They weren't laughing anymore, either.

Hissing and growling something into his ear, they shoved the roughneck back at her. He collected himself as much as he could and mounted another attack. She had to give up ground to his flurry of fists, but there was only so far she could go. His ring of rowdy friends hemmed her in and she couldn't get too close to any of them.

One of the man's punches caught her on the shoulder. She slid sideways in the dust of Main Street. It took all her strength just to stay on her feet. The man kept coming. Rosa stayed low. She kicked, catching him on the knee.

His leg buckled and the he hit the dirt with a thud. His friends were stunned silent for a moment while he writhed, clutching his knee.

"Pick him up and get all yourselves out of Thornville."

The ring of men closed in. They weren't interested in helping their friend. In fact, there was nothing friendly in their faces. This was deadly business.

She turned as the circle tightened around her. Tradi fists with one man wasn't always fun, but it was so thing she could handle. Taking on all these rough hurt and anger would go away. At least she could take it out on the hooligan in front of her.

He swayed his big barrel chest from side to side, as if that would make him a difficult target. Before he could attack again, she faked to the left, drawing his guard that way, then sent her fist into his neck, just below his jaw. Sputtering, the man stumbled backward into the arms of two of his friends.

They weren't laughing anymore, either.

Hissing and growling something into his ear, they shoved the roughneck back at her. He collected himself as much as he could and mounted another attack. She had to give up ground to his flurry of fists, but there was only so far she could go. His ring of rowdy friends hemmed her in and she couldn't get too close to any of them.

One of the man's punches caught her on the shoulder. She slid sideways in the dust of Main Street. It took all her strength just to stay on her feet. The man kept coming. Rosa stayed low. She kicked, catching him on the knee.

His leg buckled and the he hit the dirt with a thud. His friends were stunned silent for a moment while he writhed, clutching his knee.

"Pick him up and get all yourselves out of Thornville."

The ring of men closed in. They weren't interested in helping their friend. In fact, there was nothing friendly in their faces. This was deadly business.

She turned as the circle tightened around her. Trading fists with one man wasn't always fun, but it was something she could handle. Taking on all these roughnecks could be too much. Then one of them sneered and drew a long bowie knife from behind his coat. The dark, pitted blade had seen a lot of use.

He raised the stakes, but she held a higher hand. Rosa put her palm on the butt of the revolver at her hip. "I'm still the law and I say get. That means all of you and it means now."

Usually the threat of her drawing on someone was enough. There was one time when it hadn't been.

Today might turn out the same. The men still approached, now led by the one with the knife.

She was done threatening them. A bullet said a lot more than words. Rosa tightened her hand around the familiar grip of the .45. But when she tried to draw the gun, she couldn't move her arm. One of the men gripped her forearm tight. He smelled of liquor and cheap tobacco.

No son of a bitch touched her without paying a price.

She'd practiced a move for this situation. All she had to do was kick out her heels, dropping down and using her weight to break the man's grip. If it worked just right, she'd draw her gun on the way to the ground.

Rosa coiled, but someone new suddenly rushed up to her. A tall, broad man, dressed in a cavalry uniform. He cocked his fist back and drove it into the face of the man holding her. The roughneck released his grip, out cold before he hit the ground.

She finally drew her gun, but the hooligans were already fleeing, hiding among the buildings. With the immediate threat out of the way, she looked at the Army man who had come to her aid.

"Tom?"

Her blood was already pumping from the fight, but seeing him standing there, in the flesh, sent new pulses of heat through her. Was it really him? Three years had etched the lines in his face a little deeper. And his shoulders seemed wider, filling out his cavalry uniform. It had to be him. The same hunger burned in his eyes when he looked at her, and her body responded with an old burn, like someone lighting a match a mile deep in a mine.

Unlike her flesh, she wasn't so quick to forgive him.

"You lousy son of a bitch," she spat.

He tore his eyes from her to glance about the town. "The fight's still on."

"You bet your ass it is. Coming back after all this time, like you're still welcome here." Maybe her anger could overpower the attraction that seemed to tug her toward him.

"The fight with those drunken bums. They haven't left." His broad hand came toward her and she recoiled, not knowing what his touch would do to her. He was only moving the barrel of her revolver aside. She hadn't aimed it at him, but it was getting awfully close.

"I know damn well what's happening in my town. Don't need you to come back to tell me." Didn't need him to come back at all. That's what she told herself nights, after her guns had been cleaned and the lamps were all dark and she felt his absence.

"Well, you might need a hand running these fools out of here."

"You could show them the way out. I know how good you are at running." She shouldered past him, toward

"Today you do."

A metallic clicking drew their attention to the hooligans by the telegraph office fifty yards away. One man was attaching an iron box to the side of the main telegraph pole with a leather strap while the other wound a crank on its face. Once the box was secure, one man pulled a thick wire from one side, strung it around the telegraph pole, and back into the other side of the box.

Rosa turned and hurried toward them.

Tom was right with her. "That's a tree cutter."

"I know what it is. What the hell are common roughnecks doing with it on our telegraph pole?"

Damn it, she wasn't going to get there in time.

One of the men hit a lever next to the winding crank and the tension in the box released. It drew the wire tight against the telegraph pole and quickly ate into the wood. The wire continued contracting, slicing straight through the pole.

Suddenly, Tom's arms were around her shoulders, stopping her dead in her tracks.

"Those aren't common roughnecks."

With a groan, the telegraph pole separated where it was cut and the heavy top fell straight toward them.

sleepy little town anymore. Someone had to come back to keep the peace. Stick around long enough and I'll show you what I can do with a knife."

"Love to see it."

"You might be feeling it."

He slowed up a bit, allowing a safer distance between the two of them. She walked closer to the two men by the farrier's. They were huddled together, making some kind of plan. Her pistol was still out, so she'd be ready, even if one of them had another bowie.

"I think a few of them are over at the telegraph office now." Tom started to angle in that direction.

She stopped walking and Tom paused with her. Keeping an eye on the hooligans at the farrier's, she turned her attention to Tom. "You're not helping me. You left. What're you doing back? Running again? You a deserter?"

His angry blue eyes sharpened to a dangerous edge. "I earned these stripes on my arm. And the scars in my leg and shoulder from Hapsburg bullets. I ain't no deserter."

"This time."

It was a slap in the face and he showed the pain with a grimace. Good. He deserved it. And worse.

She pressed: "So what are you doing here?"

For the first time, she saw Tom searching for words. "I . . . couldn't stay away." Then that easy smile flashed across his face. Damn if that grin didn't make the air feel lighter around her. "Good thing, too. Don't see any deputies backing you."

"Don't need them." And no one had ever volunteered for the job either.

"Today you do."

A metallic clicking drew their attention to the hooligans by the telegraph office fifty yards away. One man was attaching an iron box to the side of the main telegraph pole with a leather strap while the other wound a crank on its face. Once the box was secure, one man pulled a thick wire from one side, strung it around the telegraph pole, and back into the other side of the box.

Rosa turned and hurried toward them.

Tom was right with her. "That's a tree cutter."

"I know what it is. What the hell are common roughnecks doing with it on our telegraph pole?"

Damn it, she wasn't going to get there in time.

One of the men hit a lever next to the winding crank and the tension in the box released. It drew the wire tight against the telegraph pole and quickly ate into the wood. The wire continued contracting, slicing straight through the pole.

Suddenly, Tom's arms were around her shoulders, stopping her dead in her tracks.

"Those aren't common roughnecks."

With a groan, the telegraph pole separated where it was cut and the heavy top fell straight toward them.

Chapter Two

Popping like gunshots, the telegraph wires snapped from the pole as it fell toward Rosa and Tom. He tightened his arms around her. The muscles of his body gathered up. They'd been to enough barn dances together for her to know how he was going to move, and she collected herself to follow. A second before the telegraph pole crashed into them, they sprang to the side, just out of harm's way.

The wood sent dirt and rocks flying with a thundering clap. If she and Tom hadn't moved, they'd be dead. He was right—these weren't ordinary drunken hooligans.

He was quick to his feet and helping her up. Even through the leather of her glove she felt the heat of his skin. Her body woke up to it. She suddenly sensed every bit of clothing against her skin. There was a lot of history between their bodies.

Holding onto her hand, he smiled. "Like those britches on you."

She meant to yank her hand away, but everything moved slowly, like a summer sunset. Her body needed more of his heat. Luckily, her vest was buttoned over her shirt; otherwise he'd have seen the blush she felt across her chest. The tips of their fingers lingered a moment before she was free from his touch.

"A sheriff can't have her skirts getting in the way when she's busting rowdies." The dust had cleared, and the two men at the telegraph office were gone. "Or whatever these troublemakers are."

Jaw set, he scanned the buildings for someone to fight. "They're in a world of trouble, that's what they are." If she had had no past with Tom, no scars from him tearing away from her, this man would be mighty easy to watch as he moved purposefully through her town. She had to turn away before she spent too much time staring at his determined face.

Thornville citizens peered fearfully from behind windows. No one else was out on the street to back her. Except Tom. The trouble with the hooligans had spun out of control. She was reluctantly grateful to have his help. But she couldn't tell him. She wouldn't let it be that easy for him to return. And there was no way on Earth she was going to tell him how much she thought he'd changed, solidifying from a rowdy youth into a formidable man.

Movement by the farrier's drew her and Tom's attention, and they hurried in that direction. The two roughnecks were still waiting there, ready to fight. Rosa just reached the building, when three more men jumped out from a side alley, knocking Tom away from her.

He stumbled sideways for a few steps and slammed into the side of a building. He grimaced, then smiled.

"I got these guys. You take those two." In a swift move, he launched himself off the building and into the three men.

Fists flew. Tom handled himself beautifully. He had been wild when he was younger, a troublemaker taking on all comers. But this Tom was a brutal and precise soldier. He didn't hesitate to fight and his fists were aimed for maximum impact. The men felt the pain.

Rosa almost wished she could just watch him unleashing all the power of his body, but the men by the farrier's came on quickly. If they joined the fray, the odds would turn against Tom. Rosa blocked their path.

"You saw what I did to your friend," she said. "All bets are off now that you tried to kill me."

They took one more step, then saw the .45 in her hand.

The fight continued behind her. Feet shuffled and men grunted in pain.

The roughnecks in front of Rosa looked like they wanted to join in the brawl and help their friends, but her pistol held them back. With each blow they heard behind her, they winced.

Tom was winning. "I was coming home," he growled as he knocked the men to the ground, "for some peace and quiet and good applejack and a beer or ten." One final groan and a heavy body hit the dirt. "And a nap under a tree after a blackberry pie."

She glanced over her shoulder and saw him standing over the three fallen men. He slapped his hands against his thighs, dusting them off.

Rosa motioned with the barrel of her revolver for the men in front of her to join the others Tom had corralled. They moved reluctantly, but none wanted to challenge the .45.

Tom's adversaries sat up in the dirt, wincing and holding their injuries. Tom was out of breath, but still standing. A little blood dripped from the corner of his wide grin. This was the troublemaker she remembered.

As soon as she turned her back on the farrier's building, a scraping sound spun her back around. Tom turned with her, drawing his pistol in a flash. The heavy gun rattled briefly like a snake as he pointed its four barrels at the man they faced.

The hooligan with the knife had returned, murder in his eyes. The long clip point of the Bowie was ready to strike. Rosa and Tom cocked their pistols. But the man didn't back down.

One of the roughnecks on the ground called out, "Go on, quit, Deak. They ain't paying us enough for this."

The man with the knife hissed back, "You shut the hell up. Unless you want to get the knife, too."

The roughneck on the ground seemed more afraid of Deak than Rosa or Tom.

Rosa used her voice to overpower them both. "No one's getting the knife." Her gun aimed right for Deak's heart. "Who's paying you to do what?"

Deak kept his mouth in a thin line.

Tom encouraged him. "I'd tell her before she gets mad."

The man didn't talk and didn't lower his knife.

Her patience thinned. "Someone pay you to kill me?"

Silence.

She shifted the aim of her pistol. "Drop that knife now or never use that hand again."

Tom whispered out the side of his mouth, "How good a shot are you?"

"I'll take an acorn at twenty paces. This skunk's no problem." She narrowed her eyes on the man. "You decide how much you like that hand?"

Deak breathed shallow and fast, preparing to attack. He took one step.

Rosa fired. The pistol bucked with the loud crack of the explosion. The bullet hit its mark, and the knife spun from Deak's hand. He immediately crumpled into a ball, clutching his bleeding fist.

The fight drained out of all the men. Rosa let two of them go to their injured friend, hauling him gingerly to his feet. The roughnecks were easily herded down Main Street by Rosa and Tom, revolvers drawn. Some of the townspeople came out from behind their doors.

"Get Doc Chacon," she called to Willoughby, the general store owner. "Tell him to meet me at the jail."

The hooligans groaned with defeat. One of them looked like he was going to try and make a break for it, but Tom shook his pistol, rattling it.

"You country boys ever seen a U.S. Army Rattler before?" he asked. It was a formidable weapon, black steel and brass. "Six shots of straight-up forty-four-caliber bullets from the revolver. And below, three more barrels for shotgun shells." All the barrels together formed a deadly diamond. He snarled, "Believe me, you wouldn't make it."

Willoughby hurried along the creaking boardwalks as more and more people came out. On the far side of the town, Rosa's parents were just stepping out of their leather shop. It was too far to see, but she could picture the worried and sour expressions on their faces.

Tom casually knocked his elbow against hers. "Fine shooting."

"Told you." This was far too comfortable, walking with him like this.

A flare of anger heated his voice. "So who would want you in a grave?"

"Put a few bad guys in prison, but no one with enough pull to pay for this kind of roundup." Her mind spun, flipping through faces and possibilities.

Tom seemed to be following a thread of his own. "Or maybe not you personally. They just want the sheriff of Thornville out of the way."

Only one possibility. "There's a mining company that wants claims. . . ."

"Crandall."

Was Tom caught up in all this? "How do you know?"

"Saw their rolling mining machine south of here when I was on my way into town."

They reached the front of the jail, a one-room brick building that stood off by itself. Tom kept his gun trained on the hooligans as she unlocked the heavy iron door. Usually when she threw someone in the jail, it meant the end of trouble. But it seemed like things were just starting to get dangerous.

"Where was the machine headed?"

Tom glanced to the south. He was jumpy, with the same tension she felt. "This way."

Rosa hurried the men into the jail and slammed the door shut, locking it securely. "Deak, the Doc'll be here in a minute. Put your hand outside the bars so he can work on it. Don't want you dying before you see the judge."

Deak muttered a curse back at her, but she'd heard worse on the Santa Barbara docks.

With the bad guys locked away, she walked to the center of Main Street and gazed southward. "How far away?"

"Don't know how fast that beast can roll. Day or two?"

"They've been trying to buy up plots, but no one's selling. Guess they want to take it by force." She ejected the spent shell from her revolver and replaced it with a fresh round before holstering the pistol. "Not without a fight."

She turned and headed into town.

Tom didn't follow. "Where're you going?"

"To get my horse and ride out to the Crandall machine." She hated that she still wanted him at her side. "Thanks for the help, mister. This ain't your fight anymore."

"Oh, hell." Tom squinted past Rosa, to where her parents were coming down the street. "Your folks."

He turned on his boot heel and headed in the opposite

direction. This time, she watched him leave Thornville. She thought her heart had hardened enough not to break twice, but having him come back like this, just to disappear again, was almost too much to bear. It was almost as if he hadn't returned at all. Maybe he was just a ghost, conjured by her late-night dreams and summer longings. All those wishes had been locked away so tight.

Let it hurt later. Right now she had the Crandall mine to deal with.

If she could get by her parents. They hurried across the road to the sheriff's office, where her horse was tied.

"We heard a shot." Her dad looked her over. "Are you hurt, *querida*?"

"I did the shooting." She kept moving toward her horse.

"Was that Tom Knox?" Her mother's gaze into the trees where he'd disappeared threatened to set the dry leaves on fire.

"It was."

"That *bastardo* isn't welcome here." Her father balled his large hands into fists.

"You don't need to worry." She bit back on any more emotion before it consumed her. "He's gone."

Her horse greeted her with a nicker. She checked the cinch and bridle. Might be a long ride. Her mother gripped her arm. "You'd better not be riding after him."

"I'm riding south," she explained, "to stop the Crandall mining machine that wants to chew up these hills and us with them."

"Alone?" Her father glanced south, as if he could see the threat there.

The question hit her hard. Since Tom left, every fight she'd been in, every struggle had been alone. It made her strong. She was respected. She'd had jobs many men couldn't have handled. She came back to Thornville, and was named sheriff because she stood up when no one else was willing. But having Tom next to her, just for those few minutes, felt better than old times. They understood each other, like when they'd danced together on long summer nights in hot barns and grange houses. In his absence, there'd been no balance in dancing alone. With him backing her in this fight, all the steps were that much easier. This connection seemed deeper than the desperate young passion they'd shared growing up. And now it was gone.

"Yes, alone."

A dark shadow slid across the ground, a swift bird skimming in front of the sun. But there were no wings. The shape was so strange—tall like a man in a hat—that Rosa had to look into the sky.

Her breath caught in her throat. She blinked and blinked, but what she saw was real. Tom rode through the air on a mechanical flying horse. She'd seen pictures of Sky Chargers before, lumiscopes from the front lines of the war, but never one in person. And nothing looked as impressive as Tom handling the craft, holding reins like with a horse, but levers at his feet. He took the charger over some buildings, then low to the ground, leveling off toward her.

Her parents were equally speechless—for once. Tom kept a wary eye on them as he came closer. The charger's engine chugged in a steady rhythm and the metal pieces of the mechanical horse creaked against the leather saddle and tack. Tom brought it close to Rosa, hovering at the same height as if it were a real horse.

He turned in the saddle and untied the bedroll from the back. He threw the bundle down next to the sheriff's office and put out a hand for her.

"This'll get us there faster than your horse."

She stared at his hand. "You're not trying to stop me from fighting?"

"You the law, ain't you?"

Her father ignored Tom. "If the problem is that big, go to the state authorities."

Tom was unwavering, ready.

Rosa answered he father, "State troops are in the opposite direction. The trouble would roll over Thornville by the time we got back."

"A telegraph," he countered.

"They cut the pole. Lines are down."

Tom's hand was still outstretched to her. "Let's go."

Then her mother flared. "Not with this man."

His hand curled to a fist and pulled away from Rosa. Tom turned on her mother, eyes growing cold. "I ain't who you think I was."

"You're nobody." Her mother's anger boiled up. "Father dead, mother gone. You know what happened to that shack where you lived? The blackberries took it. You don't even have any land to come back to."

Tom's mouth was a hard line. He spoke from deep in his chest, unwavering as he faced her mother. "Might not have land, but Thornville's still my home."

Rosa knew that he was right: he wasn't the same man.

Her mother seemed taken aback, but hadn't changed her mind. "You're not welcome here, Tom Knox."

"You made that perfectly clear three years ago. Even recall you threatening to call the state police and have me thrown in prison on fake rustling charges if I didn't cut Rosa out of my life."

Her mother barely listened. "It's your fault she took this terrible job in the first place."

The ice thawed in Tom's eyes when he turned back to Rosa. "I think the job fits her perfect." He looked her over, from face to star to the revolver on her hip and lower. Heat ran across her body, driven by the touch of his eyes. Whenever anyone else saw the star on her chest, they shrank away like she was the grim reaper himself. Tom put his hand out again.

Ignoring her parents, Rosa was almost ready to take it. Then she saw the ring. "Your wife won't mind me riding with you?"

A darkness flashed in his gaze, something she'd never seen in him before. He turned his hand over so she could examine what the ring really was. A bullet casing, hammered flat and curled around his finger.

"I'm married to Lady Lead. Rifle bullet, forty-five-seventy caliber."

Reaching forward, she was inches from his hand. "And that peace and quiet you wanted. Applejack and blackberry pie?"

"I saw at least twenty Whisperers guarding that mining machine. You got no deputies, no riding party, but I can see you're heading off there anyway." He was dead serious. "Ain't going to let you do it alone."

Who else had ever said this to her? Rosa reached out and took his hand. He curled his strong fingers around her, not like a man protecting a bird, but like an ally, lifting her up to fight. Using his strength and hers, she swung up to the back of the charger.

It swayed in the air, rebalancing as Tom adjusted some controls. She gripped his waist to stay on. She'd ridden plenty of horses, but none that could fly, and the sensation of weightlessness was better than anything imagined in a storybook. An uncharacteristic giggle bubbled up from her.

Tom got control of the charger and glanced back at her with a wink. "It gets better."

As her parents watched with anger and frustration, Tom kicked a lever on the horse and it rose higher into the air. Rosa held her breath. Wind whistled in her ears. Blue sky broadened all around her. The buildings and roads of Thornville shrank below. Her parents were as small as dolls, as if she could just pick them up in her hands.

Tom pulled on a pair of leather-and-brass goggles, then turned back to her. "There's a spare pair in the right saddlebag."

Keeping one fist balled in his shirt, she gingerly turned to the back of the charger. Hills and trees moved by. She finally knew what the birds felt like. When she looked down, her stomach flipped, then clenched. One hundred feet, two hundred? A long way down with nothing to stop the deadly descent. Her body went rigid.

"I won't let you fall." He reached back and patted her thigh, and quickly pulled away as if burned.

She felt the heat, too, shimmering where he touched her. It brought her back to motion. She retrieved the goggles from the saddlebag. Without the wind biting her eyes, she saw more details around her. Survey maps she'd studied of the area came alive. Mountain ranges and rivers. The bright Pacific to the west.

A glance back revealed the dollhouses that made up Thornville. "It's never been that small."

"Felt the same, coming back." He turned back toward the front of the charger. "The way it'd been on my mind, should've been a hell of a lot bigger."

"It's grown," she said. "More people coming through as jobs spread through the state."

"Only natural that Thornville would need a full-time sheriff. You get elected or did you just pin that star on yourself?"

"Little of both. I was staying with my folks when a caravan of boat builders came through on their way from Los Angeles to San Francisco." At first the town had felt lively with their presence. "They got a little drunk, got a little rowdy and no one in town was willing to stand up to them."

"No one but you."

"The crew was headed up by Theodore Lyde. The biggest and the meanest. So I challenged him when he was stinking drunk, let him wind himself chasing me, then knocked him cold with a knee to the chin."

He clicked his tongue with appreciation. "Wish I could've seen that."

"With their leader gone, the others fell in line."

"And Thornville fitted you for a star because everyone else was too scared to fight."

She tried to see the town through his eyes. A man with no family, no one waiting for him to come home. "When you were coming back, was I small, too?"

He shook his head. She noticed some scars on his left ear. A knife maybe? His skin was weathered and tough, tanned from the sun. Tom had developed into a hard man, a soldier who had obviously lived through a lot.

"Seeing you there." He spoke without turning back to her. "Fighting like that, not backing down. You were more than I ever dreamed of." Pain and loss spiked his words.

She couldn't soothe him. Her own pain still ran deep. "The Army know you have their horse?"

"No one rides this Sky Charger but me. I'm on leave from the front. Can show you the orders if you need them, Sheriff."

"I trust you."

"That the truth?" He sounded surprised.

"The sheriff of Thornville trusts you."

He nodded his understanding. "I'll take it."

That was as far as she could let it go. Somewhere ahead was the Crandall machine and maybe another fight. There was too much going on to start dragging their emotions out of the graveyard.

"What division you ride with?"

He seemed glad to avoid the deeper talk and brightened. "Upland Rangers with the Third Cavalry. We fly scout patrols and hit the flanks of big fights. Too light to take on the Hapsburg airships straight on, especially the Man O' Wars. We got armored Sky Trains and iron stagecoaches for that kind of thing."

She patted the side of the charger. Instead of feeling the smooth hide and firm muscle of a horse, her hand hit against the metal skin. "It's amazing."

"All about the ether. And thank God for that." He dove down and swooped the charger around a tall tree. "Actually, I should thank Franklin Song. He's the inventor who came up with all this stuff for us. Common water hits the tanks, is catalyzed into ether and takes us up. Without it, we'd all be speaking German and the Hapsburgs would have all our soya fields."

"Read some articles about Song. I'd love to see his workshop up in San Francisco."

"Every invention he sends to the front gives us just a little more advantage."

"But nothing like a Man O' War." That was the most frightening threat from Europe. The man-machine hybrids were a terror in battle: nearly unstoppable.

"America don't have the telumium. And good riddance." His muscles tensed. "It ain't right, doing that to a body."

"You wouldn't volunteer, if they said you had the right *aurora*, or whatever they call it?"

"Don't need it." He turned and smiled, cocky. "I'm already the best."

His confidence was appealing, but she wasn't about to feed it. "Let me take the reins."

Tom scoffed. "Already told you, nobody rides this Sky Charger but me."

She pushed harder. "I'm riding it now. Let me try the reins."

"I used to break the meanest horses in Thornville and it still took me months to learn how to control this beast. Ain't like a horse, unless you're talking about a bucking stallion balancing on a lit stick of dynamite during a tornado." He reached to the side of the charger and unlocked the top of a rifle scabbard. "Here, this is something I'm sure you can handle."

Reaching past him, her arm brushed against his leg. His muscles jumped. She yearned to lean harder into him. His body had changed, growing more rugged, as if it were cut from a quarry. But there were still traces of his old energy: a bit wild and so damn sure of himself. She'd spent the years changing as well. What would their new selves be like together? She'd probably never know. Instead, she grabbed the butt of the rifle and pulled it from the scabbard.

"Beautiful." A Gatling rifle with six barrels, a complicated and exquisite weapon constructed from iron and brass and wood. It was unbelievably light in her hands and perfectly balanced.

Tom chuckled. "Knew you'd like it."

"Can't believe they just gave you this." She sighted down the barrels at the passing landscape. "The Tom I knew would've used it to turn a whole orchard into apple butter."

"The Army doesn't *give* you anything. They *issue* it."

His voice grew flat. "The man you knew ain't around any longer."

He had changed, that was for sure. But it wasn't a complete transformation. The firebrand was still there, inside him. She'd seen it when he fought the roughnecks in Thornville. It gave her that old thrill, like they were sneaking off to Porterville again for a barn dance and late-night lovemaking. But if he was only a rabble-rouser, it would be easy to bury her attraction under hurt and anger. There was nothing easy about riding behind him, feeling his body against hers and wondering about all the potential.

"How do I shoot it?" she asked.

"That key, hanging from the chain on the stock, it winds the tension spring."

She fitted the key into the square nut on the side of the rifle. It wound like a clock, but much tighter. "Got that."

"Then you flip open the breech, back to front, and load a belt of ammo from left to right."

The steel breech opened easily. Tom took good care of this weapon. Small toothed wheels lined the bottom to grab the canvas ammo belt.

"Once she's wound and loaded," he continued, "you pull the trigger and set the whole thing spinning." He nudged her with his elbow. "Dry fire it. Got to release the tension now that you've wound it."

How right he was. But releasing the tension between the two of them wouldn't be as simple as pulling a trigger.

She brought the rifle to her shoulder again and hesitated. "It can't be this light."

Tom chuckled. "Ask Franklin Song. There's an ether tank in the fore grip. Keeps the weight down, but more important, it feeds the breech. A little ether pipes out with every bullet, lightening the air and giving you extra power and range."

He turned and moved his hand along the rifle until their fingers almost touched near the trigger. The glass of his goggles obscured too much of his eyes for her to read them, but she knew he continued staring at her as he twisted a small valve shut on the rifle.

"Don't want to waste the ether." He slid his hand back before they touched, and faced front again. "Give her a try."

Rosa steadied the rifle in her hands. Even though it wasn't loaded, she calmed her breath and gently squeezed the trigger. She'd fired guns hundreds of times, but this beast buzzed like a hornet. The barrels spun and the clockwork mechanism chattered inside. The spring slowed and the rifle came to a stop.

There hadn't been any bullets, but it was still a thrill. In her excitement she patted Tom on the back, his body solid beneath her hand. "I've got to try that with live rounds."

His smile wavered. "Might get the chance."

The weapon suddenly felt very heavy in her hands. "You've used this in battle."

"Saved my life a few times. Me and a lot of other guys." He steered the charger close to a high rocky bluff. "Saved my life a few times. Me and a lot of other guys." He steered the charger close to a high rocky bluff. Sunlight bounced from the stone and warmed the two of them.

She slid the rifle back in the scabbard. "Why would a guy running away from a fight join the Army?"

He spoke like a reflex. "I don't run from fights."

"Three years ago my parents had words with you, and you lit out without standing up to them."

He pulled his hat low and focused forward, silent. The hills passed below them. A curious crow flapped nearby, then continued on its flight. Tom watched the bird for a moment before speaking. "You make a fine sheriff."

Apologies and explanations couldn't undo what had happened, so she didn't press further. "My folks don't think so."

"They got opinions about everything."

"Especially you."

He shrugged. "They'd change their tune if they'd seen me board a Hapsburg skiff with nothing but a bowie and my Rattler."

She would like to have seen that. "You care what they think of you now?"

"There's only one person on this wide world . . ." His shoulders tensed as he cut off the sentence. "That mining machine's a few ridges ahead. Shouldn't be long."

She was as unbalanced as when she first got on the charger, with gravity gone. Words and sentences escaped her on the whistling wind. Was there another question she needed to ask? Or was there something she had to say? As if he deserved to know her. It didn't seem like anything could bring her back to stable ground.

The charger glided through the low point between two sets of hills. She squinted ahead, trying to see any trace of the Crandall machine. "You said it's straight down this way?"

"Nowhere for it to turn off between where it was and Thornville."

"That means it'll come through this notch." Several homesteads were cut into the land beneath them. "We've got to clear these people out of here."

Tom shook his head. "It'll take too long to land at each one."

"We'll go to the homesteader furthest south. That guy can collect everyone on his way back to town."

"Point the way, Sheriff."

She patted his arm and indicated the spread. "That one, butted up against the mountain."

"You know him?"

"Yes, and so do you." This was going to be interesting.

He turned back to her, cautious. "Tell me it ain't Parker."

"I'm not gonna lie."

"Shit." Tom adjusted himself in the saddle and instinctively touched his revolver in its holster. "This was supposed to be simple. Helping out the sheriff because Thornville was in trouble. Punch a couple faces. Get into a shooting fight with some Whisperers and their rotary shotguns and run the mining company out of town. You never said it was gonna be dangerous." With a heavy sigh, Tom sent the charger diving toward the homestead at the base of the mountain.

Rosa wore her .45, too. But it wouldn't come to that.

The words and nasty looks would be enough to bleed all of them. "Dangerous? It's just you, me, Parker and a little unfinished business." A lot of unfinished business. The kind that had these two men throwing punches the day before Tom disappeared. "Just like the old days."

Chapter Three

OLD TIMES BE damned. Tom wanted to start over. He'd hoped he could come back to a clean slate. Instead the past dug into him like the thorny brambles that surrounded his town.

Seeing her again after three years brought it all back. But he'd never seen her as the sheriff before. Wearing britches and a star and a gun. She took on those roughnecks without hesitation. Watching her fight that man had sent a swirl of hot and cold through Tom. This was the woman who'd been the only warmth in his heart. Eyes flashing, fists flying, black hair shining in the sun. All the plans for escape and adventure they'd planned seemed like dust. Rosa today was real, changed. She was beautiful. And he'd lost her. But that didn't mean he wouldn't help in her fight. That was the easy part. Figuring out how to take the poison out of the past was a mystery.

They got closer to the wooden house, details emerging in the joinery and expert craftsmanship.

"Parker always could put things together," Tom said. "Hell of a carpenter."

"One of the nicest spreads outside Thornville. Apples, grapes. He's talking about making wine."

"Fancy."

She chuckled, low and smoky. "I know you prefer applejack."

"We raided a Hapsburg camp one night; the officer lit out and left behind all his kit. Upland Rangers shared some good wine that week."

The charger was almost to the ground in the clearing at the front of the low, wide house. Rosa nudged his shoulder and tipped her head in the direction of a small vineyard cut into a hill. Parker was walking from among the rows toward them.

"Maybe you can give him some pointers on winemaking," she said.

It was a real established homestead, everything in its place. Just like Parker. His suspenders formed perfect lines over his unwrinkled shirt. The man waved vaguely.

Tom pulled his hat and goggles off just as the charger came to rest on the damp soil. He dismounted and put a hand out to help Rosa. Of course she swung off the charger without his aid. They both watched Parker approach. He was tall and broad, his muscular forearms showing below his rolled-up sleeves.

The stripes were still on Tom's shoulder, and the gold

cavalry braid encircled his hat. But damn, Parker could make a fella feel inferior.

Tom spoke low, out of Parker's earshot. "When I found you two at the river that last time, he was just down on one knee asking you. I was a little hasty with my fists, didn't get a chance to hear your answer. Thought you'd have married him by now."

Rosa's silence had a cold edge but the look she shot him was as hot as a powder burn.

There was a hitch in Parker's step when he recognized who stood in front of his house. His face twisted a bit, like he'd bitten into an apple before it was ripe. Just a few paces away now, he completely ignored Tom.

"Afternoon, Sheriff."

She got right to business. "There's trouble, Parker."

He bristled. "Damn right there's trouble. I need you to arrest this man." Parker pointed a finger at Tom.

It took all Tom's power not to jump Parker right there and break that finger off.

Rosa looked from one man to the other. "Arrest him? For what?"

"Horse theft."

Her surprised eyes landed on Tom. "That true?"

Tom didn't know if she was asking as the sheriff or Rosa, so he tried to calm things with Parker. "Hundred dollars. That's a fair price."

"You ain't buying your way out of this." Parker took another step forward, then hesitated when he saw the gun on Tom's hip.

Rosa maintained the scales of justice. "That's a serious accusation, Parker. You sure about this?"

"Sure as hell."

Tom just wanted to get back on the charger and find the Whisperers for a simple fight. "I ain't proud of it and I'm willing to pay for what I've done."

"You should pay with prison time." Parker's finger was still out and he came forward again like it was a sword.

"It was the sorriest filly in the corral," Tom said. "Hundred dollars three years later is more than enough."

Rosa shoved at Tom's shoulder. She was strong. "You stole a horse from him?"

"That's how I got out of town that night."

It was like getting bucked and landing flat on his back. The breath was sucked out of his body. They were all quiet. Rosa couldn't look at Tom, but Parker's eyes blazed hotter with anger. Here it came.

Parker balled his pointed finger into a fist and took a swing at Tom. It was a strong punch and would've done some damage if it had connected. But Tom anticipated it and quickly slipped to one side, letting Parker's momentum carry him past. Tom grabbed Parker's outstretched arm and twisted it behind his back.

Their feet scuffled through the dirt as Tom pushed Parker toward the house. Still holding his arm behind his back, Tom leaned hard on Parker and forced him into the hitching rail by the porch.

Rosa shouted. "Tom, don't!"

Tom growled, holding the struggling Parker. "I've

seen Hapsburg Man O' War airships and their iron centipedes level entire towns. I've put my bullet in men before they put one in me. I've seen bodies on fire, falling through the air." Parker tried to pull away, but Tom's grip was unbreakable. "I've seen the Blackfoot fighting shoulder to shoulder with the Sioux to turn back this enemy."

Rosa tugged at his arm. "Tom, this ain't the fight."

"I know that. He needs to know that." Tom wasn't ready to let Parker go. "Now I admit I done you wrong and I'll repay you for the horse, but you only get one swing at me and that was it."

Tom released Parker and shoved away from him. The other man turned slowly, still plenty of anger in him, but less fight. He straightened his shirt and suspenders.

Rosa stood between the two men, just in case. "Settle this another time. I meant it when I said there was real trouble, Parker."

He spoke through a hard scowl. "What is it?"

"Crandall mining machine is coming up this way and I need you to clear out."

Parker put his hands on his hips like he'd single-handedly stop anything from rolling over his homestead. "Ain't seen or heard anything."

Tom spoke up, hoping they could get this over with quickly. "I saw it. It'll chew right through your place."

Parker kept his eyes on Rosa. "I'm happy to help how I can, but running away . . ."

"Not asking you to run," she said. "You have to gather what's important to you and ride back to town, collecting everyone along the way. The Wilsons, Yangs, Santos and his family."

He still wasn't convinced. "A mining machine?"

Tom watched her frustration starting to percolate. "You know Crandall's been trying to buy up this whole territory," she said. "No one's sold so they're taking it by force."

Parker wasn't moving fast enough, so she put more authority in her voice. "I'm sheriff and I'm not going to let you stay here and lose everything, probably your life. Saddle up and get the rest of those people to safety. That's your job now."

Parker snapped into action, hurrying toward a small tack shed next to the corral. He threw the doors open, selected a saddle and hauled it onto the corral fence. One of the horses immediately came over, nosing the saddle and nickering excitedly.

Tom mounted the charger and Rosa slipped on behind him. Hurrying like a dust devil, Parker rushed into his house and stepped back onto his porch, buckling on a holster with a .45. He gave Rosa a small nod.

"Be careful, Rosa . . . Sheriff. And Tom, you and I will settle later."

Tom kicked a lever and the charger lifted up. He spoke when the craft was level with the porch.

"You proposed before my body'd gone cold. She's a woman with her own mind. Her not hitching up to you had nothing to do with me. It's her decision to make." He winked at Parker, pulled on his goggles and hat, and took the charger into the sky.

As soon as they were above the treetops, Rosa spoke. “Couldn’t let it alone with Parker. You already nearly broke his arm on his own property. Had to get your parting shot?”

“I wasn’t wrong. It’s your choice.”

“Couldn’t choose you. Couldn’t find you.”

There was a glimmer of hope in him, mixed with the pain of the past. Once he’d left, he could only guess what had happened to her. “Did you look?”

“I did not.” That told him everything he’d needed to know. She was a proud woman, and fierce when she wanted something. He’d hurt her so deeply she didn’t want to find him.

The glimmer of hope died. He turned the charger south and resumed their two-person campaign toward the mining machine.

But the silence wouldn’t do. Seemed like before he left, every waking minute had been spent with Rosa. Barn dances, berry harvests, and all the time they could be alone together. Sex under the stars. Talking until sunrise, making plans to sail to China or Argentina or both. Then three years of silence. He had to hear her voice again.

“Any more surprises out here? Your folks have a spread I don’t know about?”

“Scared?” She needled him and he deserved it.

“Just making sure everyone’s safe.”

She shifted behind him. It felt entirely too good having her ride with him, bodies close. “They’re in the same house, close to town. You forget your way after three years?”

“Could find it in the dark.”

"I remember. Quite a few times."

He chewed this over, liking the memory and hating how tainted it had become. Because of what he did.

She obviously wasn't ready to let it go. "Knew your way out of town in a hurry, too." Her anger was justified, and he had no idea how to make it right. "You never answered my question. Why *did* a guy running away from a fight join the Army?"

The answer wasn't in his grasp. It spun around him, high like the turkey vultures. "Lucky for you, I did." He patted the neck of the charger, then the Gatling rifle in its scabbard.

Her voice hardened. "Don't need rescuing."

"Ain't what I'm doing." Turning to her, he saw stony determination in her face.

But she wasn't cold. Her fire flared. "So what *are* you doing?"

"Helping the sheriff save Thornville. Saving our hometown."

Her eyes remained stoic. "Maybe we should deputize you."

All these damn words back and forth. Like fighting with razor blades. It wouldn't kill right away, but it hurt like blazes. And the wounds would bleed in long lines that would never close. How could he heal them? Apologize? More words. They weren't doing any good, and sure as hell wouldn't get them past where they were.

But Rosa kept slicing away. "No way you knew Thornville was in trouble when you got leave. So what were you planning on?"

He couldn't answer her or himself.

"Hope you didn't think you could come back and get me," she said. "That Sky Train left the station."

He ground out, "Thought you'd be married. Probably to Parker after that proposal by the river."

She turned the corners of her mouth down and shook her head. "Didn't have a taste for marriage after that. Didn't have any good feelings left in Thornville."

The charger sagged in the air. Tom clicked his tongue and brought the craft toward the ground. "Losing buoyancy. Got to refill the ether tanks with water."

But the conversation wasn't over. It had just started, the snap of the primer before the bullet went off.

Once on the ground, Tom and Rosa dismounted. He unlatched the auxiliary reservoir. She stood a few paces away, in the shade of a valley oak. It was the first chance he'd had to really look at her, head to toe.

Her neat britches were tucked into well-worn, lace-up packer boots. She still had the sensuous curves he remembered, hips to narrow waist. A lot of summer nights had been passed examining those curves. And in the winter, his cold hands would be warmed on her legs under her skirts. But that was the Rosa he used to know. This one was the sheriff and would probably shoot him for thinking about the soft cotton drawers she used to wear.

A buttoned vest covered her chest, but there was no doubt she was a woman, despite the shining star above her left breast. Her thick black hair was pulled back into some sort of a clip, revealing the strong set of her jaw, her full lips and high cheekbones. There was a time when she would've let him run his fingers through her hair. He ached to do it again, to watch her close her eyes, chest rising and falling with slow breaths. She'd been at the center of the only pleasure he'd known in this hard world.

If he hadn't screwed things up so perfectly, this quiet shade would've been a perfect place to take her back into his arms and kiss her.

He gestured along a thin game track, nearly overgrown with weeds. "This is the trail I took out of town."

She traced it with her eyes, north toward Thornville, then south toward anywhere else.

"Stole the worst horse from Parker's old corral and saddled it with the only property I had to my name. That mare, she's living a good life with the cavalry now, mostly pulling duty around the fort." The memories crowded to bust out of his mind. "Your folks thought I was trash. Wanted my shack torched, with me in it. They'd have tried to kill me before they let me marry you."

"We'd been running together four years, serious. There was no other man for me. All our talk of adventure and escape, it meant something. Remember? The Yukon silver mines or Canadian trading posts or starting a gambling parlor outside of San Francisco. We were supposed to make that life together." She stayed in the shadows, eyes darker than the moonless night when he rode away. "That's not worth fighting for? Instead of standing up for yourself, for us, you lit out."

"Couldn't win that fight against your parents on my

own," he shot back. "You had fun wildcatting around the territory with me, but when it came down to it with your folks, I was alone, with my back to the wall."

Her mouth was a thin line.

He turned to the charger and filled the ether tanks with water. The catalyst sizzled and the craft perked up. The chemistry of it was a mystery to him. Same as whatever was boiling up between him and Rosa. What made it better, what made it worse, he had no idea.

She stepped out of the shadows. "That thing ready to fly?"

"Yep." He swung into the saddle and she followed behind him.

Talking hadn't helped. She seemed further away than ever.

The trees drifted past as the charger rose up. They were soon heading south again. At least the trouble up ahead was simple. Shoot or get shot. Things could get real bloody real fast with the Whisperers.

"I've ridden into combat green as a river fern and barely made it out alive." He hooked a thumb toward her pistol. "You handle that forty-five nice at short range, and I see you know what you're doing with a rifle."

She was proud, but didn't boast too hard. "I keep the peace in Thornville."

"But you ever kill a man?"

Absently rubbing her trigger finger with her thumb, she took a long breath.

"It's all right," he told her. Everyone dealt with it differently. "You can check your gun if you have to."

She slid the Colt quickly from her holster, a practiced move. She half cocked it, flipped open the gate, and spun the cylinder. Her eyes remained on the pistol.

Talking about killing wasn't always simple. He understood. Handling the gun was an easy way of distracting oneself. It was a reminder that the gun was a tool and sometimes killing was necessary.

She started speaking slowly. "Alvin Bonner came through Thornville on his way to the coast. They said he had a boat there to take him to Mexico."

News of bank robber "Bonny" Bonner's death had flicked through the frontline camps like a darting sparrow. "That was you? All we heard was a California sheriff gunned him down."

"There's a no-gun policy in Thornville," she said. "He came through, and wouldn't take his off. Pretended like he didn't hear me, headed straight into Francis's saloon." She clicked through each notch in the Colt's cylinder, making sure it was loaded. "I followed him in, told him I was the law and he had to surrender the weapon. Then I recognized him. He didn't take kindly to a woman telling him what to do. And he sure as hell wasn't going to let a female sheriff lock him up. So he drew on me."

"His last mistake."

"At first Francis was steaming mad, but he changed his tune when everyone had to have a drink at the saloon where a famous outlaw was killed." She snapped the gun shut, uncocked it and slipped it back in its holster. "So now it's just a barroom tale."

"I know it ain't." He'd never imagined what kind of

woman she would become. She always had a spark, but it could've turned into anything. A forest fire that leveled the world or home fires for one man. He was in awe of this new Rosa he'd met, standing so strong, willing to fight alone.

Her distant eyes came back to him. "Won't be that bad with these Crandall men. Show them my star, have a little talk, and send them on their way."

He patted his pistol, knowing it was loaded. "They might whisper, but they won't talk."

"Then it'll be their last mistake, right?" She tried a little smile, but it faded quickly.

He held up his left hand, showing her the cartridge ring. "Before I was in the Upland Rangers. I was just a soldier with a rifle, shaking in my boots. Hapsburg centipede rolled through the battlefield one day." The screech of the iron wheels on the hard soil still rang in his ears. "Ever see one of them?"

"Illustrations in the paper."

"Won't do those beasts justice. Six round segments that can snake through almost any territory. Tetrol engines and bristling with guns. It came right at us. Only reason I didn't run was I didn't want you to get the news that I died with a bullet in the back."

"You weren't thinking about me."

"I was." None of the other men in the cavalry knew about her. He'd kept her memory locked away, but never buried. "Every damn minute. As if you were watching. Dark-haired angel up above."

"Don't play me, Tom."

"Ain't playing." He brought the charger next to a high hill, where a dry wind rustled tall brown grass. Turning in the saddle, he faced her. "Shouting sergeants and commanding officers couldn't motivate me like knowing you were watching."

"I wasn't." She pulled off her goggles to fix him with her serious eyes. "I was getting as far away from you as I could."

He tugged his goggles down and stared back at her. "Doesn't matter, does it? You still helped me get these stripes on my shoulder. You helped me through every battle. Even if you didn't know it."

"Last thing I wanted to do was help you."

"Rather see me dead?"

Her eyes darkened as she searched over him. "No."

A small victory. "Just returning the favor. You helped me, now I'm helping you." A ridge of hills separated them from where he had seen the Crandall machine. He pulled his canteen and offered it to Rosa. She shook her head, so he unscrewed the cap and drank some of the still cool river water. He tapped his ring against the metal rim of the canteen. "This soldier came leaping out of a centipede, throwing lit grenades like he was handing out candy at a parade. I didn't think, I just pulled the trigger. Saved a lot of lives with one bullet." He offered the canteen again. This time she put out her hand.

Watching her drink from where his lips had been was a new kind of torture.

She handed the canteen back. He couldn't resist taking another swig, just to get a taste of her. Maybe it was just wishful thinking, but he swore the water was laced with ripe blackberries. Her eyes never left him as he drank. The anger hadn't gone away, but there was something else there, potent and dangerous. He screwed the canteen shut, sealing away what might be their last kiss.

"You ready?" he asked.

"Let's get this done." Her goggles quickly obscured whatever emotion was in her eyes. But he still felt the energy of her body. So close, and he couldn't have her.

He pulled his goggles on and turned the charger back on their path. *Get it done*, indeed. Then what? She could arrest him for horse theft. Shoot him for wearing a gun in Thornville. She wouldn't forgive him. Any apology he made would be worth less than a dead fly on a windowsill. What the hell would an apology matter after what he'd done?

Three years ago, he couldn't make himself into an upright citizen for Rosa. Or a husband. Her folks made it absolutely clear they wouldn't accept him. Ever. He'd run instead of standing up to them and fighting to keep Rosa in his life. Stupid kid. If he could go back in time, Tom would give his old self a whupping to remember. But nothing could be undone. If he couldn't apologize with words, he'd do it with bullets.

They came over the last ridge and dipped into a valley. High mountains stood to the left and rolling hills spread to the right. Straight ahead the Crandall mining machine rumbled forward.

If flying through the air wasn't wild enough, talking with this new Tom, filling in those three years of silence, turned out to be a tornado that scattered the horizon. Nothing seemed the same anymore. They'd both changed, even in the course of the last few minutes. The anger she'd held so close, her constant companion that had replaced Tom, seemed to waver. Yes, he'd run, but he was right to call her out on not standing up to her parents with him. Only thirty-six months had passed, but they'd both seemed so much younger then. What had they grown into? Her horizon tilted and she didn't know how to right it.

But she had to pull herself together fast. The Crandall mining machine stood in stark contrast to its natural surroundings. Hard angles and iron fittings had no place in these rolling hills. Waves of heat rippled out of exhaust pipes, distorting the serenity of this remote area.

"*Dios mio.*" She'd never seen a single machine so big. At fifty feet, it was taller than any building in Thornville except the clock tower. The other mobile mining devices that had passed through town were just a little bigger than a wagon and team of six horses. This was a beast with pulleys and conveyer belts and rolling toothed wheels that could consume the local chapel without slowing down.

Tom slowed the charger, giving them time to assess the machine. She only caught glimpses of the men around it from this distance. But as Tom's posture straightened and he adjusted his pistol in its holster, her own tension increased.

"You know what they say." He spoke without turning to her. "God made man. Man made tetrol. Tetrol made man God."

As complicated as things were, she was glad to be with him for whatever was coming next. Even if she hadn't needed help as the sheriff of Thornville, having someone close who at least understood the danger and excitement would've made the world a little more tolerable. And it was clear that Tom knew just what they were getting into. As a youth, he was filled with wild abandon. Always looking for the next piece of trouble. Now he had calm confidence. But he wasn't completely stoic.

He flashed a grin, turning back toward her. "If I take out more of the Whisperers than you, you owe me a bottle of applejack. The good stuff that Harriet makes." He winked from behind the goggles.

Bravado crushed any nervousness that crept into her joints. "If it comes to it, I'll knock down more Whisperers than you. What then?"

"Name your price."

Leave and never come back. Stay and give me everything I lost when you left. "Bottle of prime tequila."

"Deal." Tom pinched the brim of his hat. "But one condition."

"There's always something with you."

"Whoever wins has to share the bottle with the other."

They stared at each other for a moment, both knowing what that meant. There were a lot of possibilities once the cork was pulled. Might be some blood spilled. Or some wild nights, days and everything in between. She wasn't forgiving him, but she wasn't locking him out either. Not when it felt like he was the only person in the world who understood who she was and didn't try to make her into anything else.

"Deal."

Tom twisted further around in the saddle and put out his hand. She shook it. Even the leather of her gloves couldn't separate her from his vitality. He felt it, too. Like they'd both gripped a lightning rod. His nostrils flared, and the muscles of his jaw twitched.

Something wicked glimmered in his blue eyes. He still held her hand, and she didn't try to pull away. "There's something I haven't done before a battle."

Tom's eyes heated as he searched over her face, his gaze finally stopping on her mouth. She felt a warm electricity pour through her. Their hands locked together. She could slap him, push him from the charger, or shoot him. She leaned forward and met his kiss.

The history of their bodies flared bright, then burned away like an old barn. This was a new fire. Their mouths joined in a searching kiss that quickly turned deeper. They breathed each other in. She felt the rasp of his stubble, tasted fresh river water. She knew his need as he pressed toward her, knew her own as she pushed back.

This fire could consume her, burning her to the ground. She might want that. Start all over with Tom. Rebuild themselves. But not now. Not with a fight looming. And maybe not ever, once her blood stopped rushing so fast and her head cleared.

She started to pull away. He broke off the kiss with

her. Their hands separated. Never had she seen his face more serious. Then a slow smile grew on his mouth.

"Blackberries."

She still didn't have a sense of a stable horizon around her. "I don't know what you think this means."

"I just want to get this fight over with so I can get into that"—he looked her face over, still smiling but with his eyes revealing a hungry need—"bottle."

She understood his hunger. "There might not be a fight after all."

He angled the charger down toward the Crandall machine. The trees whipped past them. The mining device's tetrol engines hummed high, like distant coyotes.

Tom rolled his shoulders, preparing himself. "Just keep your gun hand ready."

Flying only ten feet above the ground along a wooded path, they lost sight of the machine for a moment. Then the trees cleared and the monster loomed. Soil crunched under the heavy iron treads. Wood creaked as the whole machine swayed, lumbering forward. The armed men stationed around its perimeter walked calmly at a steady pace. They tensed, on alert, when they spotted Rosa and Tom riding toward them.

Details of the machine and the men emerged as she and Tom neared. The wood of the mining device seemed to be waxed or sealed with something that gave it a strange reptilian sheen. The men carried blackened rotary shotguns, twelve rounds to the cylinder. Ether pistols were ready in holsters. But as she and Tom came closer, the men's faces remained dark and unreadable.

Leather and brass masks obscured any features they had. Glass eyes stared blankly at Rosa. The muscles of their necks moved slightly as they whispered to one another.

Tom brought the charger close to the man in the front and tracked along with him. The Whisperer ignored them, staring straight ahead, shotgun comfortable in the crook of his arm.

"I'm the sheriff of this territory." She hitched her thumb toward the star on her vest. "I need to talk to the man in charge."

The man responded only with whispers within his mask. The other guards shifted as they walked, responding almost silently.

She tried to keep her temper level. "Obviously you're strangers, because everyone around these parts knows that I'm not to be trifled with, *amigo*."

Tom didn't seem as interested in maintaining calm. "Listen to what she says, children. She got through the roughnecks you hired without a scratch. That counts for plenty."

Only whispers came from the guards.

"Who's your gang boss? Bring him out right now," she demanded.

The Whisperers fixed their goggled eyes on her.

Tom's hand flexed over his pistol. "There's a war on and all you ore mongers care about is profits. You best take this machine somewhere else."

Rosa felt the situation could snap faster than a hammer falling on a firing pin. "I need to see your claim. You have to show me a legitimate claim, or I will turn you back."

More whispering. Their pace slowed, all walking in step. The front Whisperer's hand slipped toward the grip of his rotary shotgun. The others immediately had their fingers on triggers.

Her pistol slipped easily from its holster, cocked and ready. "Try it and all you'll be is dinner for the turkey vultures."

Tom yanked the charger to one side and drew his Rattler. "Talking's done. Lady Lead's come a-courtin'."

The Whisperer swung the barrel of his shotgun toward them and pulled the trigger.

Chapter Four

THE SHOTGUN ROARED. Heat washed past Rosa, but thanks to Tom's quick maneuvering, the buckshot missed its mark. The Whisperer twisted the grip of his shotgun sideways, rotating the cylinder to a fresh shell and fired again. She tried to aim her revolver at him, but Tom swung the charger around and put his spurs to the machine.

The charger was fast. Faster than anything she'd ever been on. She gripped Tom's shirt with one hand, the other on her pistol. They rose higher as more Whisperers opened fire. Buckshot crisscrossed the air. Her legs were tight around the charger, her jaw clamped shut. But Tom stayed loose, almost calm, as he flew. This kind of combat was not new to him.

He shouted over the din of the shotguns. "Give 'em some back!"

She tried to aim, but her barrel jumped wildly as Tom

continued his evasive flying. "How can you shoot from this?"

"Don't fight it." He stole a quick glance back. "Like we're loose with cider on a summer night. Dance with me."

The last time they'd waltzed together was in a grange hall outside of Thornville. A piano, a fiddle and a guitar had strung out the melody for their bodies to spin and glide together. Today, the only rhythm was the jarring gun blasts. But Rosa understood what Tom meant. She fell in with him, feeling how he balanced on the charger, turning his hips and shoulders.

The ride smoothed and her joints unlocked. The Colt swung in her hand, searching for a target. Still cranking the grip on his shotgun, the front Whisperer seemed determined to take them down. He was the first to fire, and he would be the first to pay.

She fired, cocked the pistol and fired again. The first bullet kicked up dirt next to the Whisperer. The next one caught him in the shoulder and sent him staggering backward into the mining machine.

Tom smiled, impressed. "Hell of a shot with a short barrel."

They wheeled in the air. The wind whistled by, cut by buckshot. It truly was like a dance. Tom aimed his Rattler with one hand while controlling the charger with the other. At just the right moment in a sweeping arc through the sky, he fired three booming shots from his revolver. One guard fell to the dirt, clutching a wounded leg.

A high whine pierced the air. Two of the Whisperers

had drawn their ether pistols and fired screaming shots at Rosa and Tom. It was enough to have the sky ripped apart by those bullets—she hated to think what a direct hit would do to their bodies.

With the long range of the ether pistols against the normal reach of her and Tom's guns, the odds tipped far against them.

Tom made a wide circle around the machine, zigzagging to avoid the gunfire. "Told you these guys wouldn't talk."

"But they'll listen." Rosa holstered her pistol and drew the Gatling rifle from the scabbard.

Tom fired a couple more shots. "Belts are in those pouches behind the left saddlebag. Unhook one and feed the rounds from it."

She yanked one of the heavy waxed canvas bags from the saddle and pulled the lead end of the cartridge belt from it. Flipping open the top of the Gatling rifle, she fed the belt into the breech, making sure all the teeth were lined up with the fabric. The gun snapped shut like a predator on prey. She wound the clockwork tight and brought the weapon to her shoulder.

Tom called back, "She kicks like a mustang."

Pulling the stock hard against her shoulder, she aimed at the Whisperers below and eased the trigger. The barrels spun, drawing the rounds in, and the first cartridge went off. It was like holding rolling thunder. Bullets sprayed. The rifle jumped in her hands. Her whole body shook, but she kept her aim steady and drove the Whisperers to cover.

The shots from the guards slowed down. She took the rifle from her shoulder to rewind the tension mechanism. Tom ejected some spent shells from his pistol and reloaded. He doubled back through the air to avoid crashing into a tall stand of trees.

"They're not stopping."

The guards might be hiding, but the machine continued on its slow and steady course toward Thornville.

She would not quit. "We have to turn them back." There was no one else to do it.

Tom didn't hesitate, turning the charger hard and diving toward the rolling machine. "Mind if I have this dance, ma'am?

"Gracias, señor."

"This time we get to choose the music."

This was what she missed when he'd left. Tom understood her and backed her all the way. Even returning as a veteran, he carried the same confidence, as if together they could make anything right. "With a beat we can kick up some dust to."

"Like something from that fancy pipe organ that fella rolled through town. Concerto in forty-four caliber."

For three summer nights the whole town had come out to listen to that Italian man from San Francisco lecture about music and play the most intricate webs of notes. Rosa had sat with Tom, hip to hip, high in a tree at the edge of Thornville.

That was peaceful. This was not. But *Dios*, did it still feel right being next to Tom again.

She swung the rifle around, preparing to fire from the left side of the flying horse. "Cut right."

"Figures you'd lead." He swerved the charger as a new barrage started from the Whisperers.

"I'm the one with the badge."

Tom made a hard move, taking the charger right, like she asked. The Whisperers lined up with the Gatling rifle's sights. One of the men had a bead on her and prepared to fire. She pulled the trigger first.

The Gatling rifle chattered, and the bullets drew a line across the polished wood of the moving machine. The Whisperer was hit just as he blasted at Rosa. He spun to the ground, dead. The buckshot whizzed past her like poisonous insects.

"Close shave." Tom switched his revolver to his left hand and fired at the Whisperers, keeping them from lining up clear shots. "You all right?"

She paused to wind the rifle again. A man lay in the dirt, dead because of her. And if she'd hesitated, it would have been her blood on the ground. The machine kept moving. There was no sign of the fight easing. "I'm right."

The machine shuddered, engines chugging harder as it lumbered up the side of a hill. The Whisperers still moved with it, finding cover around the machine and in the nearby trees. From there they took potshots at the elusive charger.

Tom kept his steady balance, as if he were racing around barrels in a ring. "Their shotguns won't carry this range. But we ain't scaring them off either."

A bullet from an ether pistol sliced up and ricocheted off the nose of the charger. Hot metal flew in shards. Tom pulled hard on the reins to get them out of the line of fire. He gritted his teeth, anger flaring on his face as he turned from side to side in the saddle, trying to find who fired.

Another shot flashed out from the tree line below. It zipped over Rosa and Tom's heads. She pointed where it came from and instinctively dug her heels into the metal flanks of the charger. "Behind that laurel."

He sped the charger low, rushing for the trees. She slung the Gatling rifle over her shoulder and drew her pistol for close fighting.

Tree trunks sped past in a blur as Tom snaked into the forest. She breathed in the cool shade. At least they had some natural cover here instead of being exposed in the air. Tom leaned lower over the charger, cranking the speed.

A Whisperer dove out of the way as they rounded a stand of scrub. He scrambled in the dirt, losing his grip on his shotgun. He whispered to the others as he crawled to deeper cover behind a fallen tree.

She tightened her grip on her pistol. "They know we're in here."

Tom didn't let up, rising up over a thick branch, then diving back toward the ground. "Good. Don't care much for shooting a man in the back."

The tall, shaggy laurel was just a hundred yards away. Tom cocked his pistol. She held hers ready. Beyond the trees, the mining machine continued to rumble up the hill.

Dark shapes of the Whisperers flitted through the forest. They moved in perfect coordination, shifting from cover to cover. The sunlight that reached through the leaves glinted off the barrels of their guns.

The laurel was straight in front of Tom and Rosa. He pulled the reins, bringing the charger up as if it were a rearing horse. The move flushed the Whisperer away from the tree, ether pistol drawn. Tom was fast, firing twice into the man's chest. The masked guard flew backward into the tree trunk then spun into the shadows.

As the charger leveled off, Rosa turned to cover their backs. Two Whisperers stepped out from behind cover at the same time. Her first shot punched through a man's shoulder. He dropped his shotgun and dove back behind the cover.

Firing again, she only managed to chip splinters from the tree where the second Whisperer prepared to fire. He barely flinched. Then a blast from next to Rosa took the man off his feet. His shot went high, buckshot tearing leaves high above her head.

She turned to see Tom, smoke streaming from one of the shotgun barrels on his Rattler. He swung around and fired again. The short barrel threw out a huge tongue of fire and smoke. Shotgun pellets rattled the low scrub and sent a Whisperer running for deeper cover.

Tom brought the charger high again. They brushed through thin branches and leaves to the sky above. The mining machine had rolled ahead, and they moved to catch up. Tom reloaded his pistol as they flew. Rosa took a moment to do the same.

He closed his pistol and spun the cylinder, checking the action. "I see you didn't take Parker's marriage offer. Any other fellows taking you for a turn on the floor?"

He had no right to ask. "This ain't the time."

"What, 'cause of this fight?" He glanced from side to side, checking for threats. "Tell the truth, I didn't dawdle with any fillies last three years. Too busy fighting the Hapsburgs. Lucky for you, too."

She didn't want to feel relief at knowing he hadn't been with anyone else. "Flattering yourself, *Señor* Knox."

"If I'd been chasing petticoats, I wouldn't have gotten so good at making war."

He *was* good at this. The charger soared higher and made a wide loop around the mining machine as it neared the peak of the hill. The Whisperers were more cautious, sticking to cover and shadows.

Hell, Tom was putting his life on the line for her and the town. The least she could do was be honest. "Played around with a dude from Santa Barbara for a bit when I was down there inspecting cargo for contraband." And it felt good to needle Tom, let him know what he'd missed.

He glanced toward the coast. His hat shaded his goggled eyes, but the sunlight showed his thin, grim mouth. "Don't tell me he broke your heart. Because I got plenty more bullets."

"Save them for the Crandall men. I broke *his* heart."

The line of Tom's mouth curved into a grin. "That's my girl."

"I'm not your girl."

The smile disappeared.

Tom put the charger into a dive toward the machine as it crested the hill. The hulking structure creaked and swayed violently. It tipped back for a moment, then surged forward onto the down slope. Once it was down this hill and on flat land, Parker's spread would be right in its path.

God protect any of the masked guards who got in her way while her blood still roiled with the echoes of her past with Tom. "If we knocked out those treads it would slow down," she said, "maybe even stop."

"Bullets won't do it. And I didn't think to pack any dynamite for a relaxing trip home."

The machine kicked up dirt on the downhill, picking up speed.

"If we can get close enough, I can jump on." She scanned the machine for some way into the interior. "It needs a body to drive it. We'll just knock him out."

"*If* we can get close." He turned the charger to double back. Their movement was tracked by the Whisperers with ready guns.

"There, on the left." A small metal ladder led from the ground all the way up the side of the machine. Several hatches along the route gave access to the inside. "That's where I'm going."

"I'll take you there." No hesitation, just action. He flew straight for the spot.

Whisperers came out shooting. The bark of Tom's Rattler and Rosa's .45 sent them back. The machine came closer and closer, the air turning hot from the engines. Because of the soya beans used to make it, tetrol exhaust smelled like frying food.

She didn't know what she'd do once she was inside the rumbling building, but at least she'd be on the ground. Last time her feet were on solid earth was in the quiet shade with Tom. Even then she didn't know which way was up.

They were near enough for her to see the metal handle at the side of the lowest hatch. There was no lock, so she'd only have to throw the latch to gain entrance. Easy, right? She cocked her pistol and fired at one more masked guard, making him dive for cover behind a rock. The wood and metal of the machine creaked and ticked. If it were an apartment building, it could have housed at least a hundred people. Instead, the insides were filled with conveyer belts and grinding wheels. And a driver to be stopped.

They were only about ten feet from the door when Tom turned the charger away sharply, nearly throwing her from the mechanical horse. He wrestled with the reins in one hand, his other reached back to keep her on the craft.

"What in hell . . . ?" she sputtered.

He didn't answer, just kept flying the charger in jagged lines away from the rolling machine. A crackling roar like a forest fire erupted behind them. Bullets fanned past, darkening the sky. It was no shotgun, or even an ether pistol.

Bouncing nimbly over the dirt track road were two iron stagecoaches. Tall metal-studded wheels ate up the ground, propelling the black carriages forward. Tetrol engines hummed with the effort of moving the metal coaches. An armored driver sat on top of each, pulling levers that kept them in dogged pursuit. And from wide slots next to the drivers, Gatling guns sent endless streams of death toward Rosa and Tom.

A FISTFIGHT WITH ROUGHNECKS wasn't unheard of. Hell, even throwing down against some Whisperers with rotary shotguns might not make the county newspaper. But iron coaches with blazing Gatling guns—that was war.

With one arm still reaching back to Rosa, Tom twisted the charger through the air, using every trick he'd learned in training and on the battlefield. He'd fought his way from death enough times to keep the boys up all night with saloon stories, but damn if he didn't hate having Rosa in the line of fire. Sure she was the sheriff and stood up strongly to a fight, but he'd do anything to keep her from getting hurt.

The bullets kept dogging them. It seemed as if these sons of bitches had experience shooting at Sky Chargers, but they'd never tangled with him directly. They'd learn some pain as soon as he got some breathing room.

"Crandall Mining must really want this territory. How much silver's in these hills?"

She pulled herself tighter to his body, balancing on the charger. "Enough to kill a sheriff for."

"You ain't dying."

After a quick dip in the air, he yanked the charger hard to the right. "We're using their machine as cover. No way they're shooting up that merchandise."

"I hate running." She still aimed her .45 at the iron coaches, as if a single bullet could do them any harm.

"This ain't running. This is circling."

The charger turned harder and the pursuing coaches couldn't keep up. They were fast, but lacked maneuverability. Tom flew behind the mining machine, and the Gatling guns finally stopped chattering.

But new gunshots rang out from the trees lining the hillside. Whisperers cranked their shotguns, sending blast after blast skyward. The Crandall guards had to dash from cover to cover to keep up with the rolling mining machine gathering speed on the downhill.

Rosa fired back at the Whisperers, keeping them pinned. "We can't circle forever."

As if on cue, the iron coaches rounded the front of the mining machine and started firing again.

"If this was a fair fight," Tom said, "we'd have ether field guns on swivel mounts that could take those coaches out." If he had just one more rider from the Upland Rangers they could even the odds.

She unslung the Gatling rifle from her shoulder and wound the action. "Don't think these *pinche cabrónes* would show up to a fair fight."

He brought them over the top of the mining machine, but the damned thing was moving so fast it was hard to keep using it for cover. The coaches continued their pursuit, machine guns firing at every opportunity.

Rosa let loose a barrage of her own from the Gatling rifle. Ether-powered bullets rained down and sparked off the metal coaches. The black steel armored plates on the drivers were dented, but they weren't hurt. And it would take a hell of a lucky shot to get a bullet through the eye slots cut into their cylindrical helmets.

She saved any more ammo and grunted in frustration. "We don't stop them, they'll take everything."

He searched the terrain for any advantage. Far ahead, some large trees grew from the side of a tall mountain. If they could knock those over . . . but how? They had no TNT or heavy artillery.

Rosa leaned tight to him and spoke into his ear excitedly. "Remember when you chased me in the forest on the other side of the river?"

It had started when they were children, innocent play. As they grew, the game became far less innocent. Beside that river was where their passion had truly started, on a warm spring night. From then on, they'd found every opportunity to meet there. "I'd be real happy to talk about those old times, or even relive them . . . after we're through not getting killed."

"Don't get your hopes up on that."

"At least another kiss when we're done."

"Listen." The fist she had balled in his shirt shook him to focus. "You thought you were chasing me, but it was always me leading you."

"To that grassy spot next to the river."

She shook him again. "So let the iron coaches think they're chasing you, then lead them into the tracks of the mining machine."

They dove low, drawing the attention of the coaches. "No wonder you're the sheriff."

Taking the bait, the coaches tore up the ground with their iron wheels, dogging him and Rosa. He kept the charger moving in a jagged line. The Crandall men weren't able to line up their sights, but they kept up their pursuit.

"That's right, you big cockroaches." Rosa's voice betrayed no fear.

Tom brought them around the front corner of the machine and pulled up quick on the reins. The charger rose quickly, then turned in the opposite direction. Below, one of the coaches couldn't maneuver quickly enough and slid sideways in the dirt before jamming under the rolling treads of the mining device. Metal ground against metal. The coach buckled, losing a wheel and getting half crushed under the rolling tread of the machine. The armored driver clumsily jumped off while the gunner from inside slammed his door open and fled. Just in time. The tetrol engine screamed for a second, then exploded, blasting into the front of the mining machine.

Groaning metal and wood lurched forward. Tom yanked on the controls, but couldn't get them away fast enough. He and Rosa were slammed sideways into the top edge of the machine. His leg and shoulder were jarred by the heavy wood. He spun around and bounced away.

Something was very wrong. Rosa was gone. He straightened the charger and saw her clinging to the side of the mining machine, over thirty feet above the ground. Whisperers were breaking cover to aim their shotguns at her. She couldn't reach the rifle on her back or the pistol in its holster without falling.

Tom kicked the charger into its fastest speed. He fired

at the Whisperers, hoping he could get to her in time. He had to. If anything happened to her, he would die killing every Crandall man and burning their machine to the ground.

She saw his approach and braced her legs to jump. Just a few feet away, he put his hand out and she leapt from the side of the machine. He gripped her arm, and she pulled herself close to his chest, facing him. With her arms wrapped around him, he turned the charger and sped away, just as the Whisperers below started shooting.

The machine gun on the remaining coach opened up, but Rosa and Tom were quickly out of range. The other coach billowed smoke. The giant mining machine tried to move over it, but the explosion had taken its toll. Metal links of the front tread sprang loose and gears spun uselessly.

Rosa laughed with the victory.

Tom looked into her fierce and beautiful face. Her arms were still wrapped around his shoulders. The noise and calamity of the mining machine receded behind them. Her chest rose and fell with her hurried breaths from the fight. He was heated, too, but it had more to do with her body pressed close to him than any gunfight. She was more dangerous to his heart than any bullet.

"Thought a lot about getting you back in my arms," he said, "but never like this."

Her eyes narrowed behind her goggles. "Told you not to get your hopes up."

"There's something I've never done after a battle either."

She kept her gaze fixed on his. All she had to do was blink and he'd pull back on the reins. Tom brought his mouth closer to hers. She had tasted like blackberries before. He was so hungry for more. Her grip tightened on his shoulders. She pulled him into the kiss.

Their hearts raced with one pulse. They breathed as one. It was a window into how powerful she really was. If she wanted to, she could take it all from him. Body and soul.

The shadows of tall trees brushed over them. They slowly pulled apart.

He licked his lips and still tasted blackberries. "I'll go into battle every day for the rest of my life if that means kissing you like that."

Shade passed over her face, darkening it. "Don't say things if you don't mean them."

"I don't." He took the charger higher, toward the peak of the highest mountain in the range. "Not anymore."

A hint of uncertainty shook her voice. "Where are you taking us?"

"Crandall machine's dead in its tracks for now, and we got to water the charger." Higher and higher, the air was clean, whipping faster across the mountaintops. "We can keep an eye on them from up here, figure out our next move. Stopped like they are, their perimeter will be set. No good for an attack. But once they're rolling again and we're ready, we might be able to find gaps in their defenses."

They disentangled themselves and she carefully slid

back behind him. The high peak came closer. It was mostly dark rock, but there were still enough trees for shelter.

She spoke, nearly a whisper, as if to herself. "You didn't forget this mountain, did you?"

"I didn't." He'd spent enough time staring up at it that he could conjure every crag and angle from memory. The same way he could close his eyes and recall Rosa from top to bottom.

The wind rushed harder as it hit the mountain and turned up. The charger wobbled through the current, then calmed as they came closer to the ground. Tom pulled off his goggles and tipped his hat back.

"Always thought the ground would be too steep to walk on up here." But there were wide ribbons of flat territory. He brought the charger among a stand of trees and eased it to the ground. Both he and Rosa sat still for a moment, breathing in the calm.

She took off her goggles and let them hang around her neck. "My ears are ringing."

He felt the bruises on his shoulder and leg from where he slammed into the mining machine. "Mine, too. You take any damage?"

She dismounted and stretched out her back with a little grimace. "Nothing that would get Doc Chacon excited." Quick and precise, she unloaded the Gatling rifle and replaced it in its scabbard. "You look like you're in one piece."

"Like a fresh-minted fifty-cent coin." He shut the charger down completely and unclipped its reservoir tank. It was light and sloshed with a little water. When he turned to look for any kind of water source, even snowmelt, he was captured by Rosa's gaze on him.

"You really take a bullet?"

He put his finger over the scar on his left thigh. "Rifle round from long distance. Never saw the fella. Could still be out there, bragging about how he wounded an Upland Ranger." He moved h is palm over his right shoulder. "This guy I got to know. Tall dude, little blond mustache. Got me with his fancy Hapsburg ether pistol."

Her face tightened, eyes fixed on his shoulder, as if feeling his pain.

He continued. "Knocked me off my charger. Thought I was dead. But I wasn't. Now he is."

The dry pine needles crunched under her boots as she stepped closer. She tugged off her gloves and placed her hand over his, still on his shoulder. Hard work had taken some of the silk from her skin, but it was the most exquisite touch he'd ever felt. In their youth, their hands had searched for and coaxed a lot of pleasure, but this was different. She was sure of herself and knew what it meant to give him just this little bit of comfort.

He had to clear his throat before speaking. "Thought this wound had healed. But it hadn't. Until now."

She took her hand away. "I can't do that."

"Too late."

Color rose in her cheeks and she cocked her head, angry. "So I get no choice? What if I don't want to help you on the front lines? What if I don't want you to heal?"

"Tell me to fly. I'll go to the state law, bring them out

here to help in the fight." It would kill him to leave her, but if her mind was made up, there was no changing it.

"There isn't enough time."

"Or you want me to stay."

"I don't . . ." Her anger seemed to waver. "I don't know who you are anymore."

What could he say that would make her trust him again? He searched for words, but it didn't seem like there was enough light in the world to help him see into the shadows of his mind. "Don't put much thought to that."

"You never did." Her eyes softened, taking him in. "Used action for words."

He missed her touch, wanted her warmth. Or a long night or a slow morning together. "Then I guess I've done all my talking." He shook the nearly empty reservoir. "Gotta find water and get the Sky Charger straight in case those Crandall men want to start up another conversation."

"There won't be water up here." She turned to look over the territory, the late day light making her glow.

"Snowmelt will do." He trudged up the hill while she stepped along the side, deeper into the trees. As she walked, she rearranged her wild hair, pulling it back into the clip.

Her words filtered through the pine trees. "I remember when we stared at this peak, imagined all kinds of things up here. Gold, howling spirits, lost tribes."

Seemed so easy to be an innocent fool back then. "Look at this—I promised you we'd come up here some day and we finally made it."

He lost sight of her but could still hear her footfalls. "Never would've guessed it'd be under these circumstances."

"Better this way than being some jackass kid who doesn't know how to appreciate what he's got." He still didn't have anything of his own but the saddle, but that didn't mean he couldn't savor every moment he could steal with Rosa.

"Get down here," she called. "Get down here, Tom."

Trouble? He drew his Rattler and hurried toward her voice, cursing himself for not reloading as soon as he'd landed. There should be two bullets in the cylinder and one shotgun shell underneath. It had to be enough. Anyone left standing he would cut down with the knife in his boot. His blood pumped cold as he rushed into the thicket of trees.

Where was she? He fought the urge to call her name. If she was in danger, he needed every advantage, including surprise. But none of that would matter if he couldn't find her in time.

Chapter Five

TOM BURST THROUGH the low branches, pistol thrust forward. If she were a villain, it would've been a terrifying sight. He was deadly quick and wasted no movements. His lean, muscular body filled out the navy blue cavalry uniform. But what really shook Rosa was the deep concern etched in his face. For her.

"It's all right." She held up her hands to slow him. "There's nothing wrong."

His eyes flicked over the clearing between the trees, searching cautiously. When they came back to her, he took a slow breath and holstered his pistol. "Sounded like trouble."

"Who could get up here?"

When he was younger, nothing seemed to scare him. Chasing her through the forest or fighting in barrooms in Porterville, he'd always had a smile. This man, though, understood loss and looked as if he'd fight to keep her.

He'd already done plenty of fighting this day. What else did he need to prove?

"Found your water."

Old snow clung to the shade next to a large jumble of rocks. Tom's body relaxed more as he strode to it with a small smirk on his face.

"Thought I was gonna have to put more men in the ground." He collected the snow in his long hands, compressing it until water flowed into the tin reservoir. Once it was full, he set it on the ground so he could reload his pistol from a leather pouch on his belt.

She took out her Colt and did the same. There was no count for how many bullets she'd fired. Crandall men fell, some might've died. It was still too early in the fight for that kind of reckoning.

With his Rattler back in the holster, Tom took another long breath. The smile came back, warming her, despite the chill in the shade. It was hard to forgive him, but it was easy to be near him. His steady gait and sure shoulders drew her body closer. They walked together back to the charger.

"I've seen other soldiers come through Thornville," she said as he opened a valve to pour in the water. "Billy Durren, remember him?"

"Sure. His folks had that apple orchard. He on the lines?"

"I think he's an engineer for Army Sky Trains. He had leave a while ago, to settle his nerves. A cloud followed him the whole time he was home."

Tom nodded. "I know it."

"There were others too. Either scared or hard like stone, dead cold."

Memories darkened his blue eyes. "It'll do that to you. Maybe these battles are only meant for the Man O' Wars. All that fire and death." He turned away, still tending the charger. "Doesn't seem like a place for a normal man."

She stood near him and without looking up, he leaned into her body, his hip on hers. Slowly, his hand slid across the small of her back and wound around her waist.

Leaning into him, she whispered, "Doesn't take much strength in the hand to pull a trigger. It takes a ton of strength to keep your humanity afterward."

He stood from the charger, keeping close to her. "It was your memory that saved me."

"I'm not a memory now."

They turned together, not quite ready to relax completely. Far beneath the mountain peak, the Crandall men tended to their machine. Hammers *ting*ed on metal and portable welding machines spat fire. Unlike normal work crews, there was no shouting over the din. They were efficient, but the damage was bad enough to keep them occupied for hours.

Rosa's breathing became slower and easier. The cool air tingled in her lungs. Every part of her was wide awake, fully aware of Tom next to her.

"We still dance well together." His voice rumbled like thunder across her neck and shoulders, down her back.

She tipped her head toward the busted mining machine. "I didn't like the band."

"Don't reckon they like you much either."

"They keep coming, I'll keep giving them reasons to hate me."

He chuckled and nodded, his voice still quiet. "Never knew you like this. You could hold a storm back from up here, pushing against the clouds."

"I wasn't always like this." She pulled away from him a bit, so she could see the late golden light glinting in his blue eyes. "Maybe I should thank you. If you hadn't run, I wouldn't have left Thornville, gotten away from my parents and learned myself."

"Can't thank me." He took off his hat and shook his head, gaze distant. "There was nothing right in what I did."

There was too much weight behind them. It was as if they were being dragged down the side of the mountain. They'd be crushed under it all.

"The past is just stories for the saloon now. What are we now?"

His gaze moved to her, searching deep into her. And he seemed to be looking for something within himself, too.

"I'm . . ." He searched for the words. "When I'm standing here with you, I'm not lost."

He drew her into him, covering her mouth with his. She gripped his shoulders, feeling the strength there. The kiss deepened, less desperate than the others they had shared before. She savored him, this man confident enough to show his need.

His hands moved across her back, along her hips. Her own wants flared, chasing any chill from the growing shadows. She had been right—the past was only memories. The two of them were new. A tremble of excitement skipped up her spine.

Pressing closer, the buckles of their gun belts clanged together. She undid hers and slid the weapon gingerly to the ground.

She felt lighter, like Tom was the only thing keeping her standing on the ground. "I only take it off to sleep and bathe."

Tom took the lanyard from over his shoulder and removed his gun belt. "I don't even take it off for that on the front lines."

Unencumbered, they closed the distance between them.

"You're not there now," she said.

"I'm somewhere much more dangerous, and I have no clue how to defend myself."

"Run?"

"Never again."

Leaning down, he brought his mouth to the side of her neck. He kissed her there, bit her skin. She wound her fingers into his shirt, pulling him tight against her chest. Her sensitive nipples hardened, needing more sensation. When his mouth found her earlobe, she sighed and laced her hand into his hair.

Pleasure had been hard to come by in the last few years. She felt herself come alive with the possibilities. His hands ran down her back and onto her ass. She swiveled forward to bring their hips together. There was no denying his arousal. Thick in his trousers, his cock stood out. She ground herself against it.

Their breath came quick. Gravity took over, as if they were falling down the mountain. No stopping them now. She unbuttoned the placket of his shirt and slid her hand inside to feel his flesh. He sighed, a broad grin on his face.

"You're not ticklish, are you?" she asked.

"Might be." The smile showed wicked intent. "Don't rightly remember feeling anything this good."

His muscles were firm under her touch, more developed than she remembered. She needed more. Tugging and pulling, they got him out of his shirt, exposing his chest to the late daylight. With just her fingertips, she drew his contours, watching him concentrate on the sensation. When she knew his body before, he was a little lanky. Perfect for barn dancing and climbing trees and chasing her through the forest until they found their hiding spot by the river. Being a soldier, going to war had thickened him. She ran her hand over the expanse of his chest, broader than she remembered. His more defined muscles all had purpose now. Her hand paused over a scar on his right shoulder, just below the collarbone.

He murmured, "Doesn't hurt anymore."

The scar was dense in the center, radiating out in a jagged spiderweb. Laced through the scar tissues were hard threads of metal. They glinted in the late daylight, like silver jewelry set in his flesh.

He saw her staring and explained: "When you get shot straight on with an ether-powered round, it burns traces of the shattered bullet into the wound. It's easier to heal around it than to try and remove all the pieces."

She shuddered. "How did you survive this?"

"Already told you, I knew you were watching."

A chill started to creep around her. "But I wasn't."

"Didn't matter. What matters is now, like you said. Maybe I thought I'd see you again." He shook his head, put his hand over hers and all thoughts of cold went away. "That ain't right: I *had* to come back. Even if you were shacked up with someone. I *had* to see you. Just to know you were alive. As long as you're alive, I am."

He kissed her cheek, her neck. His fingers stroked her hair, knocking out the clip and letting it fall free around her shoulders. She felt the muscles of his back as she gripped him. The heat of his skin made her want to burn her clothes away so she could feel all of him.

"I wasn't watching," she said softly, "but you were always there. Even miles away from Thornville. I wandered up and down the coast, throwing myself into any job I could find in order to forget you."

His mouth moved just an inch off her sensitive throat. "You going to chase me off?"

She slid her hand to the back of his head and urged him back to her. "I'm going to find out who you really are."

Hot breath singed her skin. Every nerve yearned for more. It wasn't easy taking her hands from him, but she had to get the buttons undone on her vest. Tom helped when it came to undoing her blouse. The fabric fell to the ground, yet she was still careful to not let her badge touch the dirt.

Only her flimsy chemise stood between her skin and Tom's. He moved his hands along her ribs as he leaned down for another kiss. She met his mouth just as he palmed her breast and he swallowed her soft sigh. The soft fabric of the chemise was a whispered tease, holding back the full heat of Tom's hand from her firm nipple.

She pulled away from the kiss, breathless. "Get this off me."

His smile was quick against her cheek. "Who am I not to oblige the sheriff?"

The chemise was gone in an instant. She held her breath. His hand moved back to her again. This time the calluses of his palm rasped against her nipple. The breath she'd caught was released with a moan. His skin was rough. Every ridge of his hand resonated through her nipple and breast.

She took his flames and built her own. Her flesh shimmered with it. And when he took her mouth with his, drawing her chest to his, hot, wet heat gathered between her legs.

Their breath came together, quickening. His hands skimmed down her back until he caught her hips and tugged her close. She drew her fingers along his flat abdomen until she could hook them into his belt and pull him tighter to her.

He kissed her once more, then gave a small laugh with his hands on her ass. "These britches look mighty fine on you, but they're a bit inconvenient."

"I'm not the girl I was. Haven't worn a skirt in a long time."

"Don't want what you were." He fixed her gaze with his. "I want you now."

His nimble fingers unbuckled her belt. She did the

same to his, then moved lower, undoing the buttons of his fly. The coarse wool of his cavalry-issue trousers peeled away. Beneath were simple cotton drawers. And under those was his skin.

She reached for him, but he stopped her with his hand. "Take off your boots," he said. "Spent too long thinking of you naked to rush things."

"That's all you thought about?"

He hurried to his charger and pulled one of the saddlebags off. From inside he pulled out a rolled up piece of canvas. "You know that ain't true. But they weren't all pure thoughts either." He spread out the fabric and she saw it was lined with thin wool. "Ditched my bedroll in town, but I've got this poncho."

Hopping on one foot, he pulled a boot off. After repeating the process he stood at the edge of the improvised blanket. Hand outstretched, he waited for her.

The sun had almost set into the dark blue silk sea. It cast burned gold over Tom's body. His muscles and his scars. And his eyes, wanting her. She could stop now. It would be torture to rein in the blood that surged through her, but it might hurt for him, too. And that could be her revenge.

Rosa stepped onto one corner of the poncho and leaned over to unlace her boots. They were off quickly, and Tom was at her side as soon as she stood. Their bodies came together again. Mouths joined in a kiss. Her fingers raked down his back, and he growled from low in his chest. Then he pressed forward when her hands searched lower, into his drawers.

"Rosa," he whispered. "Rosa, you have to be real, because if I'm dreaming this I'll die when I wake up."

"Is this real?" She wrapped her fingers around his rigid cock. He moaned and her own need intensified. Imagining having him inside her inspired a hot blush through her pussy.

"It can't be. It's better than anything I've known." He quickly kicked out of his trousers, now completely naked in the last light of the sun.

She stroked along his shaft, watching him concentrate on the pleasure with his eyes closed and brow drawn. His hands found her, warmed her back and palmed her breast. Drawing him closer, she held his cock against her belly. He hissed a breath as their skin seemed to ignite a new fire.

Lately, touching a man meant tossing a drunk in jail. Or maybe even a fistfight, to calm a roughneck who went too far in her town. She knew she had the strength for those struggles. But she'd forgotten what it meant to share her power with a man. Giving pleasure and receiving.

That it was Tom in her hand and against her seemed impossible. The fantasies of a young woman and the anger she'd learned as she aged were burning away. She let herself live with each new beat of her heart.

Tom placed kisses on her temple, her mouth, her neck and lower. He drew out of her hand and knelt before her. With his forehead on her belly, he hooked his fingers into her britches and slid them down. He carefully removed her britches and drawers, placing them on a corner of the tarp. The cool air was a quick contrast to her hot skin and Tom's hotter touch.

He kissed her stomach, bit her hip to send a flash of lightning through her body. His hands started at her ankles and moved up her legs. She braced herself on his shoulders. Ran her fingers through his hair. Hot breath caressed her thigh. Then his hand moved there, shaping to her curves.

"This boy ran away from a girl." His voice was so quiet, it seemed like he was talking to himself. Or praying. "Came back to a woman."

Sliding his hand higher, he brought his fingers along the inside of her thigh. She widened her legs for him. He slowed, just before reaching the core of her heat. Time seemed to stretch out, giving her every second to feel his fingers moving higher and higher. Then he slid along the wet cleft of her pussy. Time stopped altogether.

She swiveled her hips, drawing him forward and back on her. The pleasure shooting through her limbs nearly buckled her knees. One of his arms wrapped around her waist to help her stand. His chest was against her leg, and the stubble on his chin rasped along her thigh.

It drove the pleasure higher. Sensations and wishes that she'd buried for years came welling up. Too much. She could be drowned. Her hand tightened on his shoulder. *Push him away*, she told herself. But she refused. Instead of being swallowed up by all these feelings, she would let herself be carried higher with them. Higher than the tallest peak in the mountains, where they'd always dreamed of climbing.

"Don't stop," she told him. "You can't stop."

"Would never want to." He stood up with her. "Ever." His rigid cock pressed against her hip. His mouth leaned down to her nipple. His finger slid inside her.

Her moan drifted on the evening breeze. She followed it with another and another. Breath came faster as she swiveled her hips to match Tom's finger moving in and out of her. The climax built in her, carrying her even higher. He ran his tongue around her nipple and bit it gently. Currents of pleasure buffeted her. His thumb slid along her folds and rested on her clit. She lost all sense of the ground beneath her.

The climax took her. Wave after breathless wave crashed. The only sure thing in the world was Tom's hard body against hers. So much of the last couple of years was about control. Her grip on the law or the butt of her pistol. Drifting like this, on a current of pure sensation, was the freest she'd ever felt.

When her pounding heartbeat slowed and she opened her eyes, she found herself in Tom's arms. He lowered her gently to the fabric on the ground. The wool was cool, but quickly took on their heat.

A new life seemed to run through her veins. She breathed in the evening air with a long sigh. Tom stretched out next to her and ran a single finger along her ribs, her hip, her thigh.

"Never thought I'd find something like you up here."

She laughed, husky. "Lost treasure."

"Glad I didn't lose you forever." The darkening sky gave just enough light to show the depths in his eyes.

"I'm not sure you've found me." Her body needed him. As for the rest of her . . . she didn't know.

"Ain't counting on anything. I'm just going to hold on to you until you tell me to let go."

"Not yet." She traced his shoulder and arm with her fingers. "We're not done yet." Catching his wrist, she pulled his hand to her waist. He didn't need more urging to curl his arms around her and press her chest to his.

His kiss was hungry. His hands seemed to devour her, finding every sensitive spot on her body. The climax hadn't sated her. Instead she grew more ravenous with the possibilities. She wrapped her hand around his cock. He thrust forward to meet her.

He reached down and found her pussy again with his fingers. She bit his lip, and he smiled. She bit a little harder, and he slid a finger inside her. Just the tips of her fingernails dug into his cock and he growled his approval.

Grasping him at the root, she angled the head of his cock toward her. He moved his hand from inside her and grasped her hip. Their breath came deep and slow. She slid his head against her clit, circling the sensitive spot.

Her hunger grew as another climax stirred. "We don't have time to get all the way into town and break into the druggist's to steal a sheath."

"I ain't that kid no more." He turned away from her to rummage in his saddlebag, then returned with a small sealed wax paper envelope. "Army issue and vulcanized."

"Keep talking like that," she said, "and I'm going to come without you even touching me."

He tore open the envelope and rolled on the sheath.

"I could tell you all about Franklin Song's theories of negative buoyancy and how ether disrupts gravity, causing lift." Bringing his hands back to her shoulders, he kissed the hollow of her throat. "But this ain't the time for words, is it?"

Whispering *"Silencio,"* she lay back, and he moved over her.

Her pistol was within reach. Her badge shined like an emerging evening star. She was naked. Hands on his sides, she brought him closer. Her legs slid along the outside of his. She turned her hips to meet him as he brought the head of his cock to her opening.

Her mouth opened to his. Probing with his tongue, he drew hers out and they tasted each other's desire. Tightening her fingers on him, she drew him into her. Slowly, he eased through her wet heat. Filling her. She opened further to him. He plunged deeper.

There were no more words. Only breath passed their lips. His pace quickened. She ground forward to meet his thrusts. He was in her, around her. His chest pressed against hers and she felt the muscles of his arms as he supported his weight.

What she'd learned of their bodies years ago didn't count for anything. Tom was a soldier now, scarred and weathered by action. She was a sheriff, the law—and had the strength to enforce it.

She grabbed him by the shoulders and rolled him to one side. He moved easily, lying on his back so she could straddle him. Angling herself, she sat back onto his shaft, drawing him in deeper than before. They both sighed.

Taking him by the wrists, she placed one of his hands on her breast, the other on her thigh.

Then she started to grind. He thrust with her, drawing her climax closer to the surface. His hand on her thigh tightened its grip. She rode him, naked under the sky, tasting the freedom above her. He rolled her nipple between his fingers, pinched it until the pleasure sizzled in hot waves.

Faster and faster, she pressed back onto him and he pushed deeper into her. A light sweat glossed her, and she could see the sheen on his skin. She had to taste him. Leaning down, she licked along his neck, bringing his salt onto her tongue. And she drew him in to his root, grinding hard. The climax surfaced, slamming through her.

She bit into his neck, and he wrapped his arms around her back, holding her close. Her breath raced. Blood sped through her, charged with the climax. It seemed like her body would never return to normal.

When her breathing finally slowed and the rush of her pulse wasn't so deafening, she heard Tom whispering, "Rosa. Beautiful, beautiful, Rosa."

She gained enough control of her body to swivel her hips again, moving his cock in and out. He paced her, then suddenly turned them so she was on her back again. She hooked her heels into his thighs and lifted her hips to meet his. He thrust faster and harder. The dark of night hid everything but the intensity on his face. She sensed his climax building and savored how she had all of his attention.

She breathed his name, and he rippled with energy. His intensity increased until he buried himself deep inside her and froze. The climax wracked his body. His cock pulsed within her. She held him until his breath returned.

They rolled to the side, with him still inside her. A sound started deep in his chest. Was he crying? No, Tom was chuckling. It was an easy sound, like whiskey pouring into a glass.

Joining him, she felt the glow of her body stirred by the laugh. They stayed like that for a few moments. Holding each other and laughing. No doubt some owls were scared from their evening hunt by the strange people, naked and cackling on the mountain.

It was rare, making this much noise from pleasure, and she held on to the sensation. She might need to forge it into a memory right now. There was no guarantee she'd feel like this again.

Their bodies slowly separated and they lay back to look at the early stars. Distant bullet holes in a velvet curtain. Her body cooled with the night, and she curled the poncho over her. Tom shucked the used sheath and drew the wool across his body, cocooning them.

He was like a living furnace next to her. "Autumn stars are the same."

"A lot has changed." As the night darkened and her blood calmed, the questions and uncertainty came back. The answers seemed more distant than the constellations above.

"Some of it for the better."

She turned to look at him, but he was only a black shape in the night, invisible. "You still haven't answered my question."

"Yes. The answer is yes." He voice seemed to drift in from all around her.

"Don't think you remember what I asked."

"You wanted to know if I'd ever fought and killed a Hapsburg Man O' War single-handedly with only my knife against his ether pistol on the deck of his ship with the guns blazing all around us."

She played along. "I really asked that?"

"It's what everyone wants to know from me."

"In that case," she said, "to answer *your* question, yes, I did drop the entire Samson gang with a single bullet."

"All seven of them."

"From the hip."

"With your derringer."

They shared the laugh, like passing a bottle of hard cider back and forth.

He found her hand under the cover and circled her palm with the tip of his finger. "Seeing you fight, I'd almost believe it."

"Ain't too much of a stretch to have you defeating a Man O' War."

He grew serious. "What was the question you asked?"

"Why does a guy running from a fight join the Army?"

Night birds made their calls. The wind brushed through pine needles. Tom was silent. He stirred from under the poncho and felt around for his clothes.

"I'll build us a squirrel fire." His warmth left her side.

Trousers and shirt rustled. Leather pulled through metal as he cinched on his belts. He sat near her to pull on his boots. Then he was gone into the night.

She collected her clothes and drew them on. The hems and edges were chilled with the mountain air and tingled against her skin. Boots laced, she tugged on her gun belt, making sure the revolver was seated properly. Was it all gone? The flood of pleasure had passed through her. She couldn't tell if its power was destructive, or if she and Tom emerged on the other side stronger for it.

About twenty paces from the charger, Tom dug in the dirt. She picked up the poncho and followed the sound. Only a few feet away, she barely made out his shadow widening a shallow hole with a stick. He struck a match, illuminating his face for a moment. There was a great distance in his eyes, searching.

He brought the match to the small pit and a tiny fire started to crackle. It cast only a narrow pool of light. If she were just a little further away he would be nearly invisible.

Looking up as she approached, he smiled, but his eyes remained dark. "Learned these at the front. Little heat, less light. No sense in giving them something to shoot at."

She spread out the poncho for them to sit on and joined him by the fire. The warmth and living light was welcome. They pulled the edges of the poncho over their shoulders and huddled together. The answer to her question might never come.

"Thanks for the fire," she said.

"Just big enough to warm a squirrel's nuts."

"Should've brought my tiny coffeepot."

He held out a canteen, sloshing the water inside. "This'll have to do."

The metal was warm where his hand had held it. She unscrewed the cap and tasted his kiss as she drank. The water was refreshing, but didn't clear her head. Had she and Tom started up again? Started over?

She handed the canteen back to him. He took a quick sip, still deep in his own thoughts.

None of this was as simple as stopping the Crandall men from taking her town. Compared to the questions tumbling through her mind like falling oaks, gunfights against rotary shotguns and iron coaches seemed easy.

He took a long breath. "They're still working." The sounds of the repairs drifted up the mountain. "Get some rest while they ain't sleeping."

Maybe she and Tom just made the final memory of them together. It was all over, and nothing could be new again. She wanted more water to rinse the bitter taste from her mouth. They'd proved they fought well together. And her body still remembered what fires they could light when alone. But could it work now? He was still Tom Knox, the man who ran out on Rosa Campos. They'd changed, though. She didn't know if it was enough. The past was a coiled rattlesnake. Would it finally sleep or strike?

Chapter Six

UNDER A SLIVER of a moon, she had snuck out of her house and met him by the river. They'd made love, eaten blackberries and shared a bottle of beer he'd stolen from Francis's saloon. They'd talked about the Yukon, and how they would perfect paraffin cloth for rainproof coats for the prospectors and make more money than they could spend. She had slept in his arms, breathing easily, her dark hair fanned over his chest.

This night Rosa was restless sitting against him. She faded in and out of sleep, sometimes gasping herself awake. Orienting herself, she'd stare at his face for a moment. But he didn't know if she found what she was looking for there. Eventually, she'd close her eyes and drift off again.

He counted off time by the chips of bark he threw in the small fire. The Crandall men kept working, and he kept thinking about how Rosa looked on top of him, hair hanging over her shoulders as the pleasure took her. Having her, real, in his arms, was more than any fantasy he could conjure. It wrecked him.

A last taste of what he could never have because of what he'd done. Wounds that wouldn't heal. His gut twisted. He was a damned man, paying for the sins of the idiot he used to be.

Rosa woke again with a short gasp. She steadied herself and warmed her hands over the fire.

Her voice was smoky, and he tried to savor the intimacy. "You should get some rest. I'll take over the watch."

Far below them the Crandall men continued their labor. He tossed a small stone in their direction and it landed on the soft soil in the shadows a few feet away. "At least we had a better evening than they did."

She gave a little laugh, then busied herself collecting chips of bark and small twigs from around where she sat. "Sleep."

Not only was his body trained to fight from being in the war, but it was trained to snatch any shred of rest where it could. He folded his arms over his chest and closed his eyes. And he tumbled into darkness with Rosa against his shoulder.

Usually, sleeping this close to a fight, his dreams were filled with broken hammers on pistols, bullets with no primers, or ether tanks with no lift. Tonight images of Rosa danced through his mind. *Why does a guy running from a fight join the Army?* It ran over and over again in his head. She accused him with the question. She absolved him with it. It was her knife and bandage. It was her own wound, and he needed to stop the bleeding.

The surface of sleep rushed toward him. The cold night air slapped him in the face. He stretched his arms and rolled his neck, coming more awake. Rosa was still right next to him. The small fire showed the concern in her eyes as she looked him over.

"Might've been sleep, but it didn't look like rest."

He warmed his hands over the flames. "How long was I out?"

"Hour, two?"

The canteen water was icy. He took small sips and gave it to her. She drank a little, keeping her eyes on him.

"I've had mine," he said. "You can sleep again."

"Couldn't if I tried." She pressed the canteen back into his hand and he stashed it under the poncho.

"Yeah." He rubbed his hands on his face. "Don't think I want to fall back into that sleep." The sky was still and dark, but dawn might not be too far off.

She gestured toward the mining machine at the base of the mountain. "They're still working. Tried to fire it up a little while ago, but it sounded like they still hadn't fixed the treads, and couldn't get it rolling."

That was the simple fight, as straight as the barrels of his Gatling rifle. With her, the past and the present clashed with no clear battle lines. Victory seemed impossible. But he wouldn't be a coward and take refuge in the bullets and shotgun blasts below.

The words came slowly as he discovered them. "Wasn't running from the fight. Not from your parents or a commitment to you." She watched him, fire glistening off her dark eyes. "I was running from myself. I wasn't the kind of man I needed to be."

She studied him. "What are you now?"

"Ain't for me to judge. All I know is that the man I was couldn't have been what you deserved."

Her eyes continued to search his face. "Whatever you did in the Army worked. You came back a different man."

The terror of the first blast of the first cannon at the first battle still heated his blood. "Lost myself on the front lines. Had to rebuild."

"But you're not completely changed." A small smile curved her full lips. "You can still tear it up."

"Fighting's the only thing I'm good at."

She spoke in a small voice. "Not the only thing."

If there'd been much tinder on the mountaintop the whole range would've burned from the sparks that flew from their lovemaking.

"You've changed, too." He knocked the side of her boot with his. "Never saw you stand up to your parents the way you did. They ain't too happy about you being sheriff."

"I'm not trying to make them happy anymore." Her heel dug a little trench in the dirt. "It took a lot to get us to change. Like the way they use TNT blasts to shape the sides of a Sky Train's armor."

He rubbed at his shoulder. "When I was shot, I got knocked from my charger. The sky was impossibly bright. I had no breath, and didn't think I could move. Seconds felt like years that slipped by too fast. I was going to die on that spot." He broke a twig in half and tossed it in the fire. "Sitting next to you is worse."

She stilled as he continued to speak. "I fought back from the wound to live. I got no idea how to get all the way back to you."

"I . . ." She tried to corral her thoughts. "We . . ." Her smile was gone, her mouth a serious line.

He laughed, but there was little joy in it. "Wouldn't this have been easier if you'd married Parker? Sitting next to you right now is like starving to death next to an apple tree."

"I've been called a lot of things, but an apple tree . . ."

The tension drained away. It was so damned easy to talk to her.

"I think you know what I mean," he said.

"Well, you definitely didn't come back a poet."

"Fancy words won't help much with those Crandall jackasses."

"But they help to come a-courtin'."

"Didn't need them with you a few hours ago."

His blood was up. He could see just the hint of blush on her cheeks. Words might not resolve the knots between them, but their bodies were ready for more. They were already so close. A kiss was just inches away. Her lips parted. Her gaze held his. He had to taste her again.

An entirely new heat flared through him. Something was wrong. He was on his feet, Rattler in hand before he realized the sound he heard was the Sky Charger humming to life.

Rosa stood with him, pistol at the ready. She whispered, "What is it?"

"Someone here with us." He stalked closer to where the charger rested. The sky was still dark, the trees thick. He couldn't see the craft or anyone else.

"How could anyone get up here?"

"Ain't my concern right now." The charger's rear engine kicked on with a hiss and high whine. "They're stealing my horse."

What a dang fool. He wanted to kick himself for not pulling the catalyst pins from the ether tank. But Rosa was right. How *did* anyone get up there? No sense in stalking forward anymore. This was a full-on chase.

A black shape moved among the dark tree branches, only about ten feet up. Rosa hurried alongside Tom, brushing through the low scrub. Their bodies knocked into each other as they stumbled along an unseen path.

"Only take a shot if you got the man," he said. "Can't damage the charger."

"Got it." She cursed as a tree branch slapped her across the face.

Whoever stole the charger didn't have much experience on the craft. It bucked and careened across the sky, blocking the stars with its silhouette. Tom pulled a small whistle from one of the pouches on his gun belt, but before he could bring it to his lips, he kicked a large rock and flew through the air.

Black shadows spun all around him. There was no horizon, and he had no idea which way was up or down until he landed hard on the ground. A tree root slammed into his thigh. The wind was knocked from him. He lost his grip on the whistle.

Rosa shuffled quickly through the darkness. "Tom. Tom! You all right?"

Gasping a new breath, he could finally speak. "Fine. Keep track of him." He pawed through the dirt for the whistle. "I'll catch up."

Her footsteps receded toward another stand of dark trees. Tom couldn't see her or the stolen charger. Where was that damn whistle? There were rocks and twigs, and probably some animal bones, but not what he needed. Then a stick clinked against something metal, and he homed in on the sound. Finally, the whistle was back in his hand. He sprang to his feet.

He dusted off the whistle and ran in the direction he'd last heard Rosa. "You there?"

"This way." To his left, further down the hill.

"Get ready." He blew the whistle, cutting into the night with the shrill sound. There, just past a stand of trees, the charger lowered toward the ground.

Tom approached. The man on the craft panicked, trying everything he could to get the charger back in the air, but Tom knew nothing would work. The man pulled an ether pistol and started looking around for a target.

Where the hell was Rosa? Most of the shadows were too damn dark to see into.

The charger was only five feet from the ground when the man swung his ether pistol in Tom's direction. He was just bringing his Rattler around when a flash of light lit up the forest to his right.

The tongue of fire from Rosa's pistol revealed her face, stern and focused. The crack of the shot echoed loudly and the bullet slammed into the man's shoulder. He toppled from the charger and landed, groaning, somewhere further down the hill.

Tom rushed to where Rosa stood. Starlight glinted off her badge and the barrel of her pistol as she turned on him.

"Tom," he said. "It's Tom."

She blew out a sigh. "I'd kill for a little moonlight."

They moved together toward where the man fell. "Made a fine shot without it."

The charger rested on the ground, and Tom turned the engine off as they passed it.

"You whistled it down?" She patted its metal side. "Thought it was just a machine."

"Each charger has a failsafe inside, tuned to a specific whistle. When it's blown, the charger automatically lowers."

"Handy."

The hill steepened, and they picked their way slower, trying to get to where the man was moaning in pain.

"I wouldn't have needed it if I'd been smarter. These Crandall guys are crafty."

She put her hand on his arm to steady her footing. "But to get up here? That takes wings . . ."

Tension rippled through her and into Tom's body.

They both had their guns out. He squinted into the night to see what disturbed her. She leaned into him, turning his body toward something darting across the sky. Too big for a hunting owl. It was a man.

Tom tugged her toward the ground, taking cover behind a collection of mossy rocks. "Damn ether pack. That's military technology."

"Crandall's got enough money to buy anything." She cocked her pistol. "Except Thornville."

The man with the ether pack flew down below them, toward the wounded Crandall thug. Tom took a peek from behind the rocks, but it was too dark to see them.

"At least we know how they got up here."

"Not just to steal the charger." Her voice was colder than a winter wind. "That could've been to draw us out. They were here to kill me."

The thought iced his blood. "Not while I'm drawing breath."

Below, the Crandall men whispered. Clothing rustled and boots scraped on loose rocks. Then the still air was shattered by a barrage of shots from ether pistols. Green and yellow flames spit from the guns. Bullets slammed into the rocks around Tom and Rosa.

She hunkered into deeper cover. "Looks like they're trying to finish the job."

"They'll learn what that gets them." He found an apple-sized rock and pressed it into her hand. "When I go, throw this behind them."

At the first pause in the shooting, Tom broke cover to aim at the two men. The one in the ether pack carried the other straight up into the air. Rosa threw the rock and it landed with a clatter behind the Crandall men. They turned and fired into the darkness. Tom squeezed the secondary shotgun trigger. The Rattler boomed.

The thug with the ether pack yelled in pain as the pellets hit his leg. He spun through the air, nearly losing his grip of the other man.

Tom tried to keep their dark, whirling shape in his sights. "They ain't whispering now."

They swung through the sky, quickly descending from the top of the mountain and into the deep black of the valley below.

Rosa holstered her pistol. "Those two won't be back, but others will."

Tom swiveled out the shotgun barrels under the Rattler, ejected the spent shell and slid a fresh one into place. "We gotta break camp. Of course, they knew to come looking at the highest vantage."

"But we're not finding another place to hide," Rosa said. "We're taking it to them." Damn if the fight in her didn't send a hot thrill through him. "You've got my gun and anything else I can give."

They hauled themselves up the incline toward where the charger waited.

He allowed himself a little chuckle. "At least they didn't show up when we were . . ."

"Those bastards knew better. They'd have gotten shot a lot faster if they interrupted what we had going."

A quick field check of the charger showed it to be unharmed. Tom fired up the engine and swung into the saddle. She hopped on behind him, wrapping her arms around his waist for the ascent. He might make it through the battle with the Crandall Mining men, but having Rosa close without having her at all could kill him. He remembered their sex, her dark eyes at the fire, and how his words were just words and didn't seem to solve anything.

They flew up to the stand of trees that had been their brief camp. Tom dismounted to stomp out the fire while Rosa collected whatever gear had been used. In less than a minute, all the evidence of their stay at the top of the mountain was gone. It wouldn't be that easy to erase it from his mind.

Back on the charger, they skimmed just over the dark trees, using the night as their camouflage. Midway down the mountain, Tom cut the engine, leaving them only with the slight hum of the ether tanks and the gentle breeze whistling.

"No motor?" Her whisper was more intimate than he wanted.

"Gravity'll take us the rest of the way and they won't hear us coming." He steered toward a deep black notch in the hills, not too far from the mining machine. "What's your plan?"

"See how close we can get. You said a direct attack wouldn't work, but maybe a little sabotage will slow them up."

Below, a welding torch hissed with unnatural flame and someone banged on a piece of metal with a hammer. "These fools don't discourage easily."

She was harder than a cold winter rain. "They'll learn."

He brought the charger through the trees into the dark notch. They split the quiet air and landed on soft leaves. This time, Tom pulled the catalyst pin from the main tank before they started the thee-hundred-yard trek toward the mining machine.

The leaves and fertile soil absorbed the sound of their careful footsteps. Hidden in the shadows, they navigated toward the sound of the continuous work on the Crandall device.

She kept her voice no louder than a butterfly wing. "Just like when we were sneaking around in the forest as kids."

"Stalking prey is one thing." He whispered back. "But I won't sneak around that other stuff anymore. Anyone wants to know what I feel, I'll tell them. Anyone who doesn't like it can twist."

They walked on through the forest in silence. About a hundred yards from the machine, they slowed their pace. Perimeter guards could be anywhere. Tom and Rosa slipped silently from tree to tree. Fifty yards farther, the forest thinned. At twenty yards, they hid behind a large oak.

She stayed low, and he stood as they peered toward the rear of the device. A small field hospital had been set up, where several men were being tended in the light of a yellow quartz lamp. The man who'd stolen the charger was there with a bandaged shoulder. His companion sat with his back to the rear treads of the machine, his leg bound in a white dressing. Even the wounded Crandall men wore their Whisperer masks and had weapons nearby.

"Tough fellas," Tom remarked. He'd been careful to fill all the chambers in his Rattler with live ammo.

"They bleed enough to get scared off."

He gave her a pat on the shoulder, feeling the solid strength of her body. "Never said they were tougher than you."

They shifted to the other side of the tree. The main work on the mining machine's tread was being done on the far corner. Work lights cast the men's long shadows across the dirt path, revealing constant activity.

Rosa tilted her head toward another tree, and they sprinted to it. They were close enough to smell the oil and tetrol of the mining machine. It was a hulking block of darkness in the wilderness, sharp angles unnaturally blocking out the stars.

He crouched down next to her as they examined the nearest part of the machine, only about fifty feet away. "We're here. What now, Sheriff?"

"I think those are crates strapped on there," she whispered. He barely made out the dark shapes she pointed to. They lined a platform that ran all along the side of the machine. "It's the closest thing we can reach. Might help us, or hurt them if we take whatever's in there."

"It'll prove a point, too. They're not untouchable."

She smiled, showing her mean streak. It warmed him.

But this wasn't going to be as simple as taking her in his arms and waltzing the two of them to the machine, stealing whatever was in those crates and spinning away.

Two guards with shotguns walked opposite paths on this side of the machine, crisscrossing in the middle.

Her smile wavered. "They must've trained you for something like this in the Army."

"They couldn't teach me anything I didn't already know from giving your parents the slip."

It had been a long night, and the two Whisperers showed some signs of fatigue. Their heels dragged a bit in the dirt. The rotary shotguns looked extra heavy in their hands. "I'll wait after they cross, then go straight to the machine. Should give me enough time to get some crates open before they double back. Once they split again, I'm out of there."

"I ain't just going to sit here knitting," she objected.

"You're keeping watch."

"I'm coming." It wasn't a question. It was a fact.

It would be like trying to argue with the sun, telling it not to set in the west. "You slide under the machine to keep watch, I'll go behind the crates on top. When they cross again, we're running back to this tree."

"I'll go to the crates on top, too."

"Not enough room. The work on the other side's making noise to cover our tracks, but I don't want to push it."

"But if—"

He cut her off. Their timing was slipping away as the guards moved. "Unless the sheriff has snuck into Hapsburg artillery camps and busted into their ammo crates without waking anyone, I think she should stick to lookout for this operation."

"Next time I get to go to the crates."

"That's a deal."

The guards crossed on their patrol. He gave them a few paces, then nodded to Rosa. The sound of the men clanging on the metal treads at the front of the machine masked Tom and Rosa's footsteps. She reached the side of the machine and slid underneath, completely disappearing in the shadows.

Tom grabbed a wood slat at the edge of the device and vaulted up and among the crates. A quick glance to each side told him the guards weren't alerted to their presence. He had only a few moments to grab what he could. Men milled around the interior of the machine, creaking the floorboards with their steps, but there were no doors in this area, so no one could sneak up behind him.

Leather and canvas straps bound the crates to the wooden floor. Working as quietly as he could, he unfastened the latches and eased the lids open. He slipped just his fingers inside and almost hollered with delight. Opening the lid a little higher, he pulled out a satchel full of dynamite sticks.

He slung the satchel over his shoulder and checked the next crate as the guards made their turns at the far ends of the mining machine. Just a few more seconds. The second crate had several metal tanks full of tetrol and he hauled one out just before the sound would reach the guards.

Then he had to wait. Somewhere below him, Rosa hid in the shadows. God, he hoped she was safe down there. If it turned into a gunfight this close to the machine and all the Whisperers, there'd be little chance of escaping with their lives. At least Rosa would get out alive—he'd die making sure of that.

Tension coiled tighter around him as someone started to wind a hand-cranked generator. The sound came from inside the machine, like the scream of an approaching lost soul. There was trouble coming. Tom didn't want him and Rosa to be stuck there when it revealed itself. The Whisperers finally crossed, not more than seven feet in front of him. But he still had to wait. Damn it, he had to get Rosa away from the machine.

The generator hummed at full power. What was coming? The guards took a few more steps, opening the opportunity for Tom and Rosa's exit. He leapt off the machine, landing next to her as she broke cover in a dead sprint for the trees.

Just as they reached the closest oak, the power from the generator kicked in. The whole perimeter of the mining machine lit up with glaring quartz lamps. Harsh yellow light knifed into the forest. The guards looked a hell of a lot more awake, scanning the area with their glass-goggled eyes. Someone darted among the crates, knowing they'd been tampered with.

"Best not linger," Tom said, trying to catch his breath.

Rosa nodded her agreement. They rushed deeper into the trees, using the dark shadows between the yellow light as their paths.

There was no sound of pursuit. An almost giddy feeling seemed to pick Tom up and lift him faster away. Rosa was with him step for step. He handed her the metal tank of tetrol. The artificial light made her victorious smile glow like a wicked forest demon's.

They slid to a stop by the Sky Charger, where he quickly replaced the catalyst pin. It hummed to life, ready to fly. The tetrol reservoir was full enough, but the extra wouldn't hurt. He took the tank from Rosa and lashed it to the side of the charger.

She fingered through the canvas satchel over his shoulder. "I was hoping to get my hands on some TNT."

"Evens the odds a little."

They were both riding high. He felt her energy, active and ready. It was better than any of the late-night hijinks they'd pulled off before. And it was a hell of a lot more rewarding to work with her than any of the cavalry soldiers he knew. There was no stopping him. He drew her into his arms and leaned down to kiss her.

She didn't fight him. Tilting her head up, she met his kiss. They shared quick breaths for a moment, then pulled apart. A new purple light filtered into the forest, revealing the heat in her eyes.

"Careful." His voice was a rasp as he tried to control his own emotion. "We'll set this TNT off."

She licked her lips, and he wanted to fly them off to the moon so they could be absolutely alone for a year or two. "Not yet."

It felt like they were both holding onto a lit stick of dynamite, not knowing how long the fuse was. He would've loved to see where the blast took them, if not for the Crandall bastards still intent on taking Thornville.

"Ain't going to have too many places to hide now," he said, glancing at the brightening sky.

The tension between their bodies shifted as they refocused on the common enemy.

"I'll fight them in the daylight." She was the sheriff again, harder than steel.

As if in answer, the engines of the mining machine started up, rolling thunder through the valley. Its wood-and-metal structure creaked, and the treads dug into the trail with the crunching of stone. Crandall was on the move again.

Tom mounted the charger. Rosa hopped on behind him. They rose quickly through the trees. He fired up the tetrol engine, giving them more speed. But he kept a safe distance, out of range of anything but the most skilled rifleman. From the high vantage he could see the mining machine rumbling along the path, still heading north.

"*Imbéciles* don't know when to quit," she said.

"They'll wish they had after we're done with them."

He rose higher, pulling on his goggles. Rosa did the same. At this distance, he brought them to a parallel path with the machine.

She hissed a curse and pointed just ahead of the machine's path. "It's headed straight for Parker's spread."

"Can't say I'm too inspired to save it."

"Stop it with him. Parker never did anything to you."

"Except try to steal my girl the day after your parents stonewalled me. And bust my lip that time by the river."

"You broke his nose. And I wasn't your girl."

It was like a face full of snowmelt. "You weren't?"

"You never asked."

"So you whispering in my ear while we watched for shooting stars after a couple bottles of cold beer and a hot tumble in the meadow didn't make you my girl?"

She shot back. "Not officially."

"Your folks made damn sure nothing ever got official. Bet Parker was right pleased to see me gone. Probably danced a jig—"

She clicked her tongue, annoyed. "We still have to stop the machine from destroying his place."

"Guess it would be a shame if they rolled over all that nice woodwork on his house." He steered the charger in the direction of the homestead.

"Get us close, I'll throw the dynamite at the machine, and slow it down or blow it up completely."

He shook his head. "They can shoot farther than we can throw a lit stick of TNT. We'll have to think of something else." The machine picked up speed. "And we have to do it fast. They're closing in, and time is running out."

Chapter Seven

THE DEMONIC MACHINE was designed to eat through mountains in search of gold and silver. How the hell was Rosa supposed to stop something like that? The rectangular monster lumbered on, closing in on Parker's land. Armed Whisperers still walked along with it. The remaining iron coach chugged nearby, Gatling gun poking out of the firing slot next to the armored driver.

She felt too small, even sitting on the flying charger with Tom. They were just a speck in the sky. But she wouldn't be helpless. She'd taken on and won other fights. No one else in this territory wore the sheriff's star.

"Take us to the side of the mountain," she said, "by that tree and rocks."

Tom steered the charger toward a huge tree that angled from the mountain next to Parker's homestead. Around its base was a collection of silvery gray rocks and boulders.

He nodded. "I see what you're cooking up."

"We're enlisting Mother Nature."

The sky continued to brighten. The horizon was still deep blue over the ocean, but the tips of the mountains started to show with golden light from the east. Birds woke, darting among the trees. The air stirred to life with a cutting, cold breeze.

Speeding ahead on the charger, she and Tom made it to Parker's spread before the mining machine, but its steady progress would get it there soon. Circling the large tree on the side of the mountain, she looked at the height, trying to gauge where it would fall.

Tom drew a line from the tree to the mining machine's path with his hand. "If we put down enough of a blast, we could set the tree just about there, at the edge of the vineyard."

"The rocks would go with it, too, blocking their route. They won't just eat right through it, though?"

"Not with all the saws and grinding wheels folded up like that. They're tightened down for travel now."

She patted the thick bark of the old tree. "Shame to lose this tree, though."

"I'm sure Parker'll build something real fine with the wood."

He set the charger down behind the tree, and they climbed onto the steep incline. Small rocks slipped away from under her feet. She nearly slid down the hill with them. Tom put a hand out, and she grabbed it to steady herself. Joined together, they both nearly toppled the fifty feet down the slope.

Exactly right, she thought as she collected her footing. Tom coming back could bring a much needed touch to her life, or he could spin them both to ruin.

She let go of his hand and pulled three sticks from Tom's satchel of TNT. "We need blasts on the front and back of the trunk. Gravity should do the rest."

He started to climb down toward the front of the tree. "Set the top, I'll place these."

Amazing that something as small as these paper wrapped cylinders could set off such an explosion. But she'd seen the potential of TNT when it was used to blast a hillside for a local road. She put the sticks at the base of the tree, snuggled halfway into the dirt. The fuses were about two feet long.

She called down to Tom, who was hidden in the last remaining night shadows. "How short should I cut these fuses? How fast do they burn?"

He came back around the tree, dusting his palms on his thighs. "No idea."

"So we could light them and be blown to bits before we're back on the charger?"

"We're not lighting them. We're shooting them."

He put his hand out again. She took it without hesitation. Together they climbed back up to the charger and mounted it. They pitched back into the air, circling around the tree. Further up the path, the mining machine continued its trek. It would be there in less than a minute.

Tom unholstered his pistol and cocked the hammer. "I'm taking the charge at the front. You take the back."

She took out her Colt and tried to steady her aim. Her heart beat faster as the mining machine approached.

Tom spoke through a clenched jaw. "We've got to do it now. At the same time, so the blasts hit with full force."

"Give me a count."

"How about you just give me a little squeeze with your thighs when you're about to shoot, I'll fire with you."

"They teach you that in the Army?"

He quirked a wry smile. "New tactic. You inspire me."

"Get ready."

"Ready." His pistol was balanced evenly in his hand.

She aimed hers, not fighting the movement of their bodies on the charger, but swaying with it. The machine drew closer. Some of the Whisperers spotted her and Tom. They readied their weapons. The remaining iron coach sped up the path to get an angle on the charger.

A deep breath steadied her hand. She squeezed her legs against Tom's hips and pulled the trigger. His shot boomed just a split second after hers. The bullets streaked to their targets. The dynamite exploded.

Fire blossomed around the tree in a deafening blast. The concussion pushed the charger away, and chips of wood and stone rained down on her and Tom's shoulders. The tree groaned, falling toward the bottom of the slope. The rocks detached with it, avalanching through the low shrubs toward the path of the mining machine.

The driver of the iron coach reacted first, veering wide to avoid the coming danger. The Crandall device was less nimble, but slowed with the screech of reversing engines. And just in time. The tree lanced across its path, rocks tumbling nearby to break up the terrain. Whisperers ran out of the way, some getting lost in the rising dust of the commotion.

Tom whooped at their success. "That should do it."

He was right. The Crandall men didn't look very interested in spending the time to deploy all the teeth of the giant machine simply to saw up a tree and break some rocks. Instead, the Whisperers at the front quickly searched out a way around the homestead.

Rosa ejected the spent shell from her pistol and loaded a fresh round. "Parker owes us the first bottle of wine he makes."

Tom reloaded as well, quick and efficient. "He owes us a whole barrel."

The mining machine swiveled on its treads, making a wide turn to avoid the debris in its path. The iron coach still darted around like a deadly black spider but it was out of range for now.

Kicking the Sky Charger back into motion, Tom kept them tracking along with the Crandall machine.

"So, why didn't you go with Parker?"

"You think you deserve an answer?"

The young sun flashed on his goggles, hiding his eyes. "That's for you to decide."

The Tom she used to know would talk about Parker with a cold sneer. Parker had land, a family tied to the area, a vocation. Everything Tom couldn't claim. This Tom, though, didn't seem to be asking out of spite, or fear that Parker could lure her away. He was asking about her, not the other man.

"I didn't need a carpenter," she said. "I can hang a door myself if I need to."

"I don't doubt it. But there are things a body doesn't want to do alone."

"He's going to make a nice girl a good husband. But he's not the kind of guy to put up with his wife being sheriff."

Pinching the brim of his hat politely, Tom grinned. "You need a fella who shoots his gun the same time you shoot yours."

The rush of the shot and the blast still ran through her. Even the hot pulse of blood through her veins since their sex hadn't gone away completely.

"We *need* to keep track of the machine," she countered. "Parker's spread is safe, but Thornville is still dead in its sights."

He straightened his posture, becoming the soldier again. "Any more nature we can throw in its way? Still have some TNT."

"Nothing close enough to its path. Couple more hills and it'll be into town."

He scratched his chin, considering. "If we can mosquito them for a while with potshots and quick raids, it might chip away until a bigger opening . . ." Without another word he veered hard in the sky, turning the charger and speeding in a new direction.

Shots rang out behind them. Bullets buzzed past, whistling with ether. She pulled out her own gun and tried to see their attackers, but only saw slim shapes against the rising sun.

"Ether packs." Tom grunted as he twisted the charger evasively through the air. "Sneaky bastards came out of the sun. Caught a whiff of their catalyst at the last second."

"I didn't smell anything." She tried to aim at the fleeting figures, but Tom was swinging the charger too wildly to line up the sights.

"Their ether's different from Army issue. Ours smells like carrots, theirs smells like burnt potatoes."

A bullet whizzed by, far too close. She shot back at the attackers, just to give them something to think about. Now that Tom mentioned it, she did smell something akin to roasting carrots. But she wasn't tuned like he was to pick up on the enemy's scent.

He was busy steering and barely glanced back. "You get a shot?"

"Trying. They're still against the sun."

"Hold on."

She gripped his shirt tighter as he plunged the charger into a steep drop. Her stomach sank as the world twisted all around her. The ground rushed toward them. Bullets sped past. Then he took a hard turn and pitched straight up. Two Whisperers wearing ether packs sped past them, overshooting the chase. For the first time she was able to see the contraptions. Two black tanks lined their backs, with a small tetrol engine in the middle, powering a fan. Leather straps held this all on their shoulders and each man manipulated a control cable with his left hand to steer.

Tom steadied the charger for a heartbeat. "They're yours."

One man lined up in her sights as he turned to attack them again. The sunlight flashed across his goggles. He wouldn't be able to see her and Tom. She squeezed the trigger and sent a bullet streaking into the Whisperer's ribs.

He dropped his ether pistol and it dangled beneath him on a lanyard as he spun in the air, hand pressed to the wound. The other flying Whisperer opened fire again and Tom swerved out of the way. Rosa fired back, but her shot went wild. She cocked again and tried to steady her aim.

"At least we're not shooting into the sun anymore," she said.

Tom had his Rattler out, looking for a target. "These Crandall dudes know their business."

The steady chatter of a Gatling gun started up beneath them. The iron coach was dogging them from the path below, ahead of the mining machine. Tom yanked them away from the spray of bullets.

Rosa hissed in frustration. "They have more men, more bullets." It seemed like the mining machine would roll forever, crushing Thornville and everything else in its path. "What the hell do we have?"

"How many of those roughnecks did you take on in town?"

The question wasn't going to help anything. "I don't know."

"Exactly. You weren't counting. You just stepped into the fight. And you didn't quit until it was over." He fired at the flying Whisperer, sending him for cover behind a tall tree. "So take the rifle, and give them sons of bitches on the ground something back."

"Gracias." It was all she needed. Nothing ever came easy. And fighting was what she'd grown to know best.

But as she reached to pull the Gatling rifle from its scabbard, a single shot slashed through the trees and went straight into the undercarriage of the charger. The small craft bucked, and Tom quickly tried to adjust the controls. Rosa fired her pistol in the direction of the shot, but only caught a glimpse of the Whisperer with the ether pack.

Tom cursed, and cursed again. "This is going to get rough."

"What do you—"

Something in the charger hissed loudly and the craft shot forward with incredible speed. She nearly tumbled off the back, but grabbed onto Tom's belt at the last instant. Her muscles burned as she pulled herself closer to him, fighting the forces against them. Green trees and brown hills streaked past. The river flashed with sunlight, then was gone behind them.

They flew out of range of the iron coach's machine gun. They had traveled so far and so fast, she couldn't even see the mining machine. It seemed as if they'd sped over miles of territory in just a matter of seconds.

The charger's hiss turned to a rasp and Tom manipulated more controls. He spoke through clenched teeth. "Going down."

Descending fast, the charger broke through the trees. Leaves and moss clung to Rosa and Tom as they were battered by thin branches. The ground came closer and closer. She felt Tom put all his strength into steering the charger, angling them toward some soft soil. But it wasn't going to be soft enough.

Rosa whispered, *"Madre . . ."* Then they hit the ground.

The front of the charger dug in, pitching the back forward. Tom flew off to the left. She'd been thrown from enough horses to know not to fight the fall. Angling herself to the right, she tried to tuck into a ball so she didn't land face-first in the dirt. Her back crashed hard into the ground and she rolled, gasping for breath.

Bright sky and dark earth flickered as the world spun and spun. She finally came to a stop, putting her hands out and sliding just at the base of a thick tree. Her breath burned back into her lungs. Shaking her head, she quieted the dizzying whirl that blurred her vision.

Her first words came out in a croak. "Tom. Tom."

"Told you it was going to get rough." He waved from a patch of grass about twenty feet away. "You hurt?"

She flexed her fingers, tested her joints. "No." Bruised but not broken. "You?"

He pulled off his crooked goggles and staggered to his feet. "Nothing a slice of berry pie wouldn't fix."

Leaning on the tree, she tested her legs to see if they would support her. It took a moment, but she was soon back on her feet. "I don't bake."

"Maybe I do." He dusted his hat off against his leg and walked to the charger. A wince tightened his face as he rotated his shoulder, but it didn't slow him down.

One step, and Rosa knew something was wrong. She

shifted her balance and discovered her pistol was missing from its holster. Pacing away from Tom, she kicked through the leaves and grass until the gleam of the barrel caught her eye. Feeling complete with the Colt in her holster, she returned to Tom.

He crouched next to the charger, running his hands over the metal panels. Lifting some of them up, he inspected the inner mechanisms, clicking his tongue with disappointment.

"How bad is it?" She couldn't see any damage on the exterior.

"Could be worse. Ain't good, though." He glanced at her and hooked a thumb toward her pistol. "Gotta make you a lanyard for that sometime."

"Can the charger fly?"

"Ether tank's punctured. We were venting out the bullet hole. That's why we were going so fast." He unhooked a saddle bag and laid out a tool roll. "Might be able to patch the hole. If the catalyst isn't damaged, we can refill the tank with water and fly."

"And we won't know if the catalyst is damaged until we fill it."

"You got it."

"Well then, get to patching." She pulled the water reservoir and unscrewed the top. "Unless you want to bake a pie instead."

Shaking his head with a little laugh, he placed some tools in a specific order. He poured powder from a tin into a small metal plate. "Give me a splash of water here."

She poured a little into the powder and he stirred it

with a brass spatula. After a few seconds, it thickened into a paste.

"Patch it up," she said. "Let's get back at them."

"Gotta keep stirring it until it changes color."

She couldn't see the mountains to the east, let alone the mining machine. "They're moving ahead, and we're how many miles away? We don't have time to be sitting around here."

"If I don't do this right, we're not going anywhere." He kept stirring. "Believe me, I'm itching for some payback."

The scraping of the spatula in the metal dish was like a clock counting down to a midnight hanging. Tom finally seemed satisfied and returned to the charger. He reached inside and spread the gray paste on the ether tank's bullet hole. The smell of hot metal rose, like in a blacksmith's shop. The edges of the patch sizzled a little as it burned into the steel around it.

"Franklin Song, I tell you." Tom cleaned his tools on the grass. "Man's a genius."

"At least he didn't make any monsters, like that Italian lady did. If she had her way, science would be the new religion, with everyone going to laboratories to pray."

The paste stopped sizzling and Tom unclasped a valve behind the saddle's cantle. "Give it a fill. We'll see what happens."

Water sloshed into the tank, followed by a low hum. But Tom's face didn't brighten as the charger rose a bit from the ground.

"Hear that buzz?"

It sounded like a single bumblebee trapped in the tank.

"We'll fly," he continued. "But not at full strength."

She reattached the water reservoir and pawed through his saddlebags. One of them had a coil of thin rope and she cut off a length with the jackknife she always kept in her left front pocket. "But we'll fly enough to catch up." She tied the rope into a loop and attached one end to the trigger guard of her Colt, slinging the rest over her shoulder.

Tom finally smiled, admiring her work. "I'll carry you there if I have to." He swung into the saddle and put out a hand.

It wasn't necessary, but she took it anyway and mounted the charger behind him. She settled her legs against his. He took them up, and there was no adjustment necessary. They fit together well and balanced effortlessly on the craft. Rosa's world had gotten so twisted around that Tom, the man who'd ran out on her on a moonless night, was now the surest thing in it.

She placed her hand on his shoulder and leaned toward his ear. It was bold, but what the hell. "Heading into another battle."

Hunger flashed in his eyes when he turned to her. "Don't mind if I do." Everything disappeared as she closed her eyes.

All she knew was his kiss and the buoyant feeling of rising up through the air. His lips moved over hers, as if searching for the same security and strength she did. They found it together.

Ending the kiss, they pulled apart and collected themselves for the next round of the fight. He was right: the Sky Charger didn't feel like it was at full power. It sagged a bit, keeping them close to the treetops. They pushed forward toward the jagged line of mountains.

She craned her neck, but still couldn't catch sight of the Crandall device. "How far are we?"

"Couple of miles, I reckon. But the bigger question is, you still going to let me kiss you once the battle's done?"

Even though they flew ten feet over the tops of the trees, at a pace faster than a horse's trot, the question swirled around her and wouldn't go away. Part of her wanted to answer yes. Most of her, in fact. But the opposing voice was loud. Was it weakness? Falling right into her old life with Tom, as if he hadn't broken her heart? But neither of them was the same anymore. Before, he'd been like a coyote without a pack: lean and hungry, always looking for trouble with restless eyes. Now he was more like a mountain lion. Determined and steady. There was no way back for either of them. If it was the real Tom with her now, fighting and sharing heat and sex. There might be a life ahead of them.

"They've got Gatling guns," she said, "an iron coach, rotary shotguns and men with ether packs. A kiss can't be the only thing on your mind."

He cocked his head, considering. "It is."

"You'll get a kiss when we win."

"Then you know I'm going to do everything I can to win."

"I'm counting on it." She relied on him. It felt good, having someone to lean on.

He checked his pistol and loaded fresh bullets.

She did the same, testing the grip of her gun now that it was tied to the lanyard. The Gatling rifle waited in the scabbard. Clockwork, breech, trigger. She ran through the process of loading and firing it. The satchel held enough TNT to do some damage. The Crandall men were well armed, but so were they.

Tom maintained his focus ahead. "You happy I'm back?"

She remembered what he'd said about how she helped him in the war, as if watching. "I'd hated you so much in those three years." When his mouth tightened into a scowl of regret, she continued. "I spent so much time trying to forget you, it just proved I never could. Looking back, I'm glad I could help you at the front. I'm glad you lived."

"So, you happy I'm back?"

She'd built a lot of walls around herself. Then she had to push against them to keep the structure from collapsing. And if it did, she'd be crushed. She stopped fighting the press, letting the walls fall past her as she stepped forward.

"*Sí*," she finally said. "I'm happy you came back."

A long breath drew the tension out of his body. He rolled his shoulders like a pugilist preparing for another round. "Those Crandall boys ain't. Gonna make them pay for hurting my charger."

"They picked a fight with the wrong town." She fought the urge to dig her heels into the metal flanks of the craft. "If Thornville's still there."

"There's the machine."

She followed his outstretched hand and saw the black rectangle moving among the distant trees. It was climbing the last hill before town. Once it hit the downslope, there would be nothing to stop it.

"*Más. Más.* Faster," she urged him.

He pulled his goggles on. "I remember what you mean when you say, '*Más, más.*'" The charger lurched forward. He kicked another lever and they picked up more speed. "Pace ain't the problem. It's lift."

They brushed the treetops just underneath them. The charger couldn't climb over some of them, and they slapped at her and Tom's shins. The wind whistled past. Rosa covered her eyes with the goggles. Three playful birds darted up from the forest and kept pace with her and Tom. He noticed them, too, but barely gave them a glance. The birds flew close for a moment, but veered away, quickly disappearing into the green blur below.

Tom gave a laugh. "They recognized us."

"Don't tell me you're in touch with the spirit world now."

"You saw how they skipped out," he said. "They knew what we are."

"Which is?"

"Predators."

He was right. The two of them were focused forward, heading toward a fight. "I never asked to draw on someone," she said. "I didn't want it."

"It wasn't your choice," he said. "Mine either. Hapsburgs attacked our country. Crandall Mining attacked your town." The charger sped faster. He leaned low, weaving through the treetops. She pressed into his back. "But we ain't prey," he continued. "We're the hunters."

An animal grin took her. The birds had scattered. Everything should get out of her way. Anyone who stood and fought her would be cut down. The mining machine came closer, and she felt that joined like this with Tom, their determination alone should burn it to ash.

They broke out of a group of trees and into a clearing. The mining machine was about a mile away, cresting the last hill before Thornville. The iron coach still patrolled the path ahead, and the Whisperers were small dots around the perimeter.

"Get us there," she urged Tom.

He snaked them through the next set of trees, then swung as high as the charger could climb. The mining machine lurched on the hill and started down the other side, picking up speed. The sounds of its engines doubled, echoing through the valley. Something was happening.

Tom gritted out, "Sons of bitches."

"Dios."

The front of the machine started to unfold. It looked like a poisonous insect's black limbs and sharp talons. Huge rotary saws and conveyer belts and grinding wheels stretched forward, ready to consume whatever got in its way. Just ahead of this ravenous beast lay the town of Thornville.

Chapter Eight

MAN-MADE TEETH AND claws were more terrifying than anything nature could devise. As they flew closer to the mining machine, Rosa saw the details of its destructive power. The rotary saw was at least ten feet in diameter. Nothing could stand in its way for long. Debris would fall on a churning conveyer, drawing it toward two offset grinding, spiked wheels. Their steel teeth gnashed together, ready to crush. From there, the unlucky victims of the machine would be drawn into its center, for sifting and sorting, she presumed.

"That first building still the stable?" Tom leaned low over the charger and tipped only his head in the direction of town.

"Yeah. They added on to it last year to accommodate iron coaches and their mechanics."

The Crandall machine's engines screamed, heat shimmering in waves from the exhaust tubes. Metal ground against metal, and the rotary saw started spinning, singing like a chorus of demons. It was only about twenty yards from the stable.

The two main doors to the stable swung open, and Parker waved all the horses out.

"At least Parker came through," Tom said

Ears pinned back, the horses pounded away on panicked hooves. The din of the machine swallowed Parker's shouting, but he was inside the building with no idea how close the saw blade was. If he didn't get out of there soon, he'd be consumed by the ravenous metal mouths.

"Get out of there, Parker!" She yelled as loud as she could, but her voice didn't reach far enough.

Tom pulled his Rattler and fired a wild shot toward the machine. It didn't do any damage, but it did catch Parker's attention. Rosa waved wildly for him to run. Parker finally peeked out the doors of the stable and bolted, sprinting as fast as his legs could take him.

"Good man." Tom slowed the charger a bit and started to circle the machine, about two hundred yards away. "But we also let them know we're here."

The Whisperers ignored Parker to track the Sky Charger's movement, weapons at the ready. The iron coach motored away from the machine, giving it space to maneuver and fight.

A horrible screech tore the air. The saw blade chopped into the side of the stable, splitting the wood and scattering splinters. Shaking more than any earthquake she'd seen, the structure groaned and buckled. The saw continued as the mining machine moved forward. The walls and supports were ripped apart. Debris fell onto the conveyer belts and sped into the waiting metal teeth. It was worse than she imagined. A timber the size of a man was quickly reduced to dust.

She shuddered with the destruction. "At least the horses are safe."

"It'll take weeks to collect them out of the hills and forest."

"Now it's the people we have to worry about."

All the commotion had driven the citizens of Thornville onto the streets. Some ran around haphazardly with fear. Others were frozen in terror, merely standing and watching the machine as it ate through the stable.

The iron coach started firing, and Tom swerved out of the way. He grunted in frustration as he circled around the mining machine. It was two thirds of the way through the stable and would be on to the blacksmith's shop next.

"The problem is that you're too good a sheriff." He fired his rattler at a Whisperer who was bringing his shotgun around to bear. The man dove away, unhurt. "Keeping the citizens safe, so they don't know how to fight for themselves."

"It's never supposed to get this bad." She slid the Gatling rifle from its scabbard and used the key to wind the mechanism. "This is worse than any nightmare."

He ducked them low, under the aim of the iron coach. "After getting into the war, I started looking forward to my nightmares for a little relief."

The ammo belt snapped into the Gatling rifle. She tried to steady her breath and brought the weapon to her shoulder. But aiming at the iron coach was nearly impossible as Tom flew in his erratic, evasive pattern.

"Set me down." A quick glance around the town told her there was nowhere safe. "I can't line up from up here."

"Remember dancing the waltz with me?" He reached back and gave her leg a quick squeeze. "Put your hips into it."

Everything seemed to slow down. She allowed the movement to take her again, rather than fighting it. The rifle was an extension of her, sights zeroing in on the iron coach. A pull of the trigger set the rifle into quick action. The barrels spun and bullets flew, charged with the ether.

A line of dents appeared on the side of the coach where her shots hit. More bullets sparked off the driver's armor. He veered away, disappearing between two buildings.

"It didn't stop them," she said, "but I scared them."

He flashed her a brief smile. "You're dancing great."

"To be honest, it wasn't dancing I was thinking of."

Tom brought the charger to an abrupt stop and fired his pistol twice. A Whisperer fell backward, firing his shotgun into the air as he went down. Tom took the charger higher again. "Keep at the iron coach. You'll get a shot into the slot eventually and hit the gunner. He's the one we really need to worry about."

There was no sign of the coach in the town.

"Where the hell is it?" she demanded.

"Could be on the other side of the machine." He started to bring them around the device as it finished consuming the stable. Its heavy treads crushed any part of the structure that wasn't ground to dust inside the machine. The blacksmith's shop and everything else in town would go that way if they didn't do something soon.

She just caught sight of the iron coach when a sense of danger flared through her like a thousand lit matches. And it all started with a smell.

"Potatoes."

Luckily, Tom knew just what she meant and jerked the charger to one side as a bullet whizzed past them. Two Whisperers wearing ether packs streaked out of the sunshine. They were damn close. Tom swerved again so they couldn't get a shot off with their ether pistols.

"At least the iron coach's Gatling can't shoot at us while they're up here." He turned his head from side to side, trying to track the flying Whisperers, but they were moving too fast for him to shoot.

"But the mining machine ain't stopping." It rolled toward the blacksmith's, surrounded by the armed Whisperers. The townspeople backed further and further away, helpless to defend their property.

"Now might be the time for that TNT—"

His sentence was cut off as a flying Whisperer blindsided them, slamming into the charger. She fought to stay on the craft and tried to grip Tom, yet he was ripped from her hands.

But he didn't fall. He was lifted higher, locked in a struggle with the flying Whisperer. Leaving her alone on the charger.

"Whoa! Whoa!" She instinctively called out, but the machine paid no heed. It spun wildly, unbalanced and unpredictable.

It was a challenge just to move forward into the saddle while slinging the Gatling rifle over her shoulder, but taking up the reins didn't solve her problems. Tom had been right—this was no ordinary horse. It was like trying to sit astride a dust devil. There were two levers at each of her feet and a set of valves at the base of what would be the horse's neck. Yanking the reins, she managed to slow the spin a bit, but the bottom of the craft swung from side to side, threatening to throw her.

And there was still a Whisperer with an ether pack trying to catch her. If she did lose control and fall to the ground the impact might end her, or the guards below would. Tom continued to speed away with the other Whisperer. All she could do was pull the reins, kick the levers and hope to slow things down enough to pull her pistol and shoot back at all the men trying to kill her.

TOM HAD BEEN in enough fights to know how to punch a man. But to do so while dangling thirty feet over the ground was another matter altogether. Both he and the Whisperer had lost their grips on their pistols, and they dangled on their lanyards. The other man was strong, his fingers digging into Tom's shoulder as he tried to shove him off.

"Best give up your fight now, before you get hurt." Tom jabbed his elbow into the man's ribs, but the mask obscured any expression of pain.

Every passing second burned Tom. He could only steal glances, but knew Rosa was alone on the charger, whirling through the air as she struggled to control it. Either she'd crash or make an easy target. He had to get to her. Now.

But the Whisperer had no intentions of making this easy. He brought his knee hard into Tom's side, nearly knocking the wind out of him. Tom grabbed the control lever for the ether pack and twisted it, sending them into a tight spin. As the Whisperer struggled for control, Tom was able to get a hand free and balled it into a fist. It was a quick uppercut, without a lot of room to develop, but it felt good planting it on the man's jaw.

The mask flew off while the guard was in mid-whisper. Tom's spine froze. The man wasn't speaking English. His words came out in a stream of German. It all made sense. The advanced weapons, the military technology.

"You're a goddamn Hapsburg."

The man's eyes went wide, shocked to be found out.

Tom cocked his fist and punched the man in the face. But the Hapsburg soldier maintained his grip on Tom's shoulder. And somewhere below them, Rosa still twirled, barely controlling the charger. He had to get to her to tell her that these weren't ordinary evil mining company goons—these were soldiers and saboteurs.

The man spit German words out, trying to dislodge Tom. This fight wasn't going anywhere, and time was in short supply. Letting the soldier punch him in the ribs, Tom tried to ignore the pain and reached down to his boot. His hand wrapped around the oak handle of his bowie knife, and he drew it from the sheath.

Sunlight glinted off the blade. The soldier fought

harder to push Tom away. The man was obviously trained in combat and blocked Tom's wrist, keeping Tom from stabbing him. But Tom wasn't trying to cut him. Instead, Tom dug the edge of the blade into a leather strap that held the man to his ether pack.

The strap split. The man slipped downward, but caught hold of the very bottom of the ether pack. Tom wrapped his hand in the leather strap and kicked down into the solder. The man's grip broke. He fell away from Tom and the ether pack. Thirty feet later he hit the roof of the hotel and lay there, motionless.

Tom sheathed his knife and wound himself into the remaining ether pack strap. It was off balance and awkward, but he was able to grab the control lever and take himself toward Rosa.

She seemed to be doing better on the charger, leveling it out. Riding it was one thing. Riding and fighting was a whole other skill. The remaining Whisperer in the ether pack orbited her, trying to get a shot off with his ether pistol.

"Right heel slows her down," Tom shouted to her, still not close enough to help.

The charger's bucking eased. Rosa swung around in the saddle and took a shot at the man in the ether pack. The bullet barely missed him. She cocked her pistol and fired again. This shot came even closer, and the man had no interest in testing her a third time. His tetrol engine whined. He sped away, slipping to safety on the other side of the mining machine.

Lurching in the air, Tom managed to get about ten feet over Rosa and the charger. "Steady her," he called down.

"What do you think I'm trying to do?"

"Clear the saddle." He had to time this perfectly. The charger slid back and forth beneath him and he swung, barely hanging onto the ether pack. Rosa shifted backward. He had to make his move now.

He held his breath and let go of the ether pack. It slipped quickly up and away from him. Falling free, he tried to aim for the moving charger. His boots hit the saddle just as the craft turned away. He nearly bounced completely off the charger, but at the last second he managed to get a leg over the saddle.

Rosa lurched forward, gripping his shirt. His fall halted, together they righted him in the saddle. The charger calmed under his control. They were soon flying straight and level—making them the perfect target. Shots chattered as the iron coach came around from the other side of the mining machine. Tom steered the charger evasively.

Still gripping him close, Rosa spoke over the din of the machine gun. "You're gonna have to teach me how to ride this thing."

"That was lesson number one. Did mighty fine. Better than me the first time."

It felt like he was fighting a headwind, but other than the bullets, the air was calm. Damn ether tank damage was making the charger sluggish. A quick glance to his fuel gauge didn't boost his morale, either.

He searched for a safe place to put them down. The Whisperers were out in the town, breaking windows and scattering the citizens. Screeching with smashed wood and crushed metal, the mining machine ate into the blacksmith's. There was nowhere safe.

"Gotta land." A small pocket of quiet behind one of the fruit cannery buildings looked like the best place. "Need fresh water and tetrol."

She let go of him and unslung the Gatling rifle to fire back at the iron coach. Her bullets pinged against its side. The driver yanked on his levers, turning the metal wheels and kicking up dust in the opposite direction.

It bought Tom enough time to make a straight approach from behind the building. But things weren't quiet for long. A group of five Whisperers charged through the area, firing their shotguns into the high windows of the cannery and flushing out some townfolk from their hiding places.

Most of the people made it to the safety of the forest, but two of them were exposed, and they hesitated at the edge of the thorny blackberry brambles. Rosa's parents.

"Dios mio." She opened up with the Gatling rifle at the enemy. Dirt flew and the Whisperers ducked for cover behind crates and nearby trees.

They were still ten feet off the ground, but Rosa wasn't waiting. She swung off the back of the charger and landed with a roll. Part of Tom wanted to just watch her incredible body and fighting spirit. But this wasn't the time to be idle.

She ran, firing at a Whisperer behind a crate, until she was next to her parents. Tom brought the charger down fast, landing hard next to a tree and pulling his pistol. Firing twice on the run, he tried to pin down the Whisperer behind the crates. Tom waved Rosa over to a large tree and tried to shoot at a guard who came around the side of the canning building.

Click. Tom's gun was empty. He sprinted for the tree just as the Whisperer opened fire with his rotary shotgun. One blast missed, shredding the air just behind Tom. The next shot dug into the tree as Tom ducked behind it.

"Did you hit any?" Rosa and her parents squeezed behind the tree with him.

He quickly reloaded his pistol. "No. You?"

She wound the clockwork on the Gatling rifle. "Not yet."

Tom gave her father a quick pat on the back and pinched the brim of his hat for her mother. "Howdy, *Señor* and *Señora* Campos."

They pushed through their fear to smile weakly back at him. Her father could only manage, "*Hola*."

"Still mad I'm back?"

Rosa shot him a look. "This ain't the time."

He stole a glance around the tree and saw a Whisperer break cover to join the other one behind the crates.

"But we're here, all cozy like." He holstered his pistol, and Rosa handed him the Gatling rifle. "Two at the crates. That means there's three more running around."

She nodded, checking her pistol to make sure it was completely loaded.

He continued to her parents. "It's funny. If you'd asked me three days ago when I was setting out from the front, I'd have told you I was coming to Thornville because it was home. But that ain't right. Like you said, I got no property, no claim. I came here because Rosa's here."

A blush glowed on Rosa's cheeks. He felt his own heat rising. Damn if, in the middle of all this, he didn't want to find out how far across her body that blush traveled.

He had to clear his throat. Speaking like this was easy. The bullets were flying, and there was no time to think. "Now, I don't know if she'll have me, but it's my intention to spend every minute I'm not fighting at the front with her. And there ain't a thing you can do to change my mind."

Shotgun blasts rang out and leaves shuddered free from the tree. On the other side of the building, the mining machine continued to chew into the town.

Rosa shook her head, unbelieving, at Tom. "I told you this wasn't the time."

He readied the rifle. "I'll cover you to the crates, and hold 'em down."

She nodded and they both took a deep breath. Before they broke cover around opposite sides of the tree, her father grabbed her arm and her mother placed her hand on Tom's shoulder.

Her father spoke first. "Be careful, *querida*."

"I'm doing my job," she said. "Better than anyone else."

Her mother shook Tom, emotion showing in her eyes. "We have to trust you now."

"I'll shoot straight. I'll keep her safe." But there were no guarantees. Any second could bring death.

This time, when they danced, Tom followed her lead. She gave a brief nod, and he swung around the tree, aiming the Gatling rifle at the crates where the Whisperers hid. He sent a stream of lead into the wood, keeping them pinned. Rosa sprinted away from the tree, rushing the crates.

Fluid and graceful, she really was a predator defending her territory from evil. She fired once with her pistol, cocked it and fired again as she neared the crates. Tom broke cover and ran toward her. She leaned down and picked up a rotary shotgun from one of the fallen Whisperers.

Just in time. The other three Hapsburg soldiers came out shooting. One of them burst out of the forest on Rosa's side. Tom had to face the other two in the opposite direction as they sped around the corner of the canning building.

He unleashed the rifle, taking out the two men. Rosa's shotgun blasted behind him, and he knew she took care of the Whisperer on her side. There was a brief moment of quiet. He quickly wound the clockwork in the rifle. She collected a shotgun shell bandolier from one of the fallen men and slung it over her shoulder.

"They're Hapsburgs," he told her as her parents cautiously approached from behind the tree.

Her eyes went wide. "Crandall Mining is hiring Hapsburg soldiers?"

"Don't think they're Crandall. More like saboteurs, trying to win the war the underhanded way. Shaking the morale of the people. I've heard of them trying to distribute fake newspapers in cities, just to scare the citizens."

She cracked open the shotgun and reloaded the spent

chamber. "That's no way to fight a war. This is our home." Anger radiated out of her, and Tom almost pitied the enemy. "There'll be no mercy for those Hapsburgs."

He picked up another shotgun from the ground near the crates and handed it to her mother. "Hold this area."

She nodded, determined.

Taking her father over to the charger, he pointed out the necessary valves. "Fill her with water and tetrol."

"You got it." Her father was already working on the machine when Tom rejoined Rosa.

They readied themselves at the corner of the canning building. The din of the mining machine continued. Engine whining, the iron coach still patrolled somewhere out in the town. And there were still Whisperers on foot.

He gave her a wink. "Three steps and we're back in the battle."

There was a vicious gleam in her eye. "They're playing our song."

They came around the building and rushed into the fight.

THE MINING MACHINE was impossibly large. A mechanical god bent on destruction. She hadn't seen it from ground level in the daylight. The beast seemed to loom all the way to the clouds.

The blacksmith's shop lay in smoldering ruins. The farrier's next door was quickly being chewed to pieces. After that was the telegraph office. Anger welled in her, fueling the fight. It wasn't a greedy mining company, it was the enemy of the whole country trying to destroy Thornville.

"If we don't stop them, they're going to roll over every small town in their way."

Tom hadn't strayed from her side. "Trying to break our backs. Setting fires through the country that could lead to anarchy. Cowards aren't battling on the front line."

There were no Whisperers between them and the mining machine. She ran toward it, hoping there were enough shotgun shells to destroy every last piece of the technology. Peeking out from above the device, the remaining Whisperer with the ether pack readied his pistol.

But he didn't attack.

Tom turned in the street, searching. "That ain't good."

Engine screaming, the iron coach sped around a corner and bore down on them. Metal studded wheels flung dirt into the air. She slung the shotgun over her shoulder. Tom grabbed her arm to pull her back, but she tore out of his grip and dove forward.

Her timing had to be perfect. Instead of being crushed by the tall wheels or having the nose of the coach smash her body to dust, she rolled under the vehicle. It passed over her, only about a foot above. Heat from the engine blasted like an oven. Just as the coach was about to clear past, she grabbed onto the rear hitch and was yanked along with it.

She had a vague sense of Tom rushing after her, shouting her name, but she was too concerned with holding on for her life to pay much attention. Her shoulders burned, fingers ached. Gritting her teeth, she pulled herself along the chassis. A final effort brought her boots up from skipping against the dirt. She curled herself onto the rear of the rolling machine.

She saw Tom running toward her. He had the rifle ready, but couldn't take a shot with her there. She motioned to him that she was planning on heading up. He nodded just before a bullet struck the ground next to him.

Tom turned his attention to the attacking Whisperer with the ether pack, firing the Gatling rifle into the air. He ran and dodged as the Whisperer snaked through the sky, shooting back. Safe for a second behind cover, Tom waved her on.

The coach bounced hard on tight springs, making her grip each handhold tightly as she climbed up the back. If she lost her grip, she'd be back on the ground. The driver wasn't making it easy on her. He swerved hard to the left, swinging her out then slamming her hard into the metal sidewall when he swung back.

Oh hell, he was bringing the vehicle around so the gunner could throw lead at Tom. She hauled herself higher until she stood on the roof of the coach. Crouching low for balance, she slowly walked forward, unslinging the shotgun.

The armored driver caught sight of her and tried to draw a pistol. But he was weighed down by the metal encasing his body, and she was faster on the trigger. Her first blast punched a huge dent in the armor. One crank of the handle brought the next round to the chamber, and she fired, putting the shot in the gap between the armor's arm and shoulder.

A yell of pain echoed within the armor. The driver pitched forward and fell off the coach. Clanging loudly, the rear wheel rolled over his metal chest. The coach bucked hard and Rosa tumbled forward. She hit the deck, nearly losing her grip on the shotgun and sliding off the edge.

But she managed to scramble into the driver's seat and took the levers into her hands. The charger had been like trying to harness a whirlwind. Despite the speed and power of the coach, the controls made sense. She slowed the vehicle and swerved to keep Tom out of the gunner's sights. She saw the barrels of the Gatling gun shifting in the shooting slot below her feet.

"I'm driving this time, Tom," she shouted to him.

He sent a spray of bullets toward the flying Whisperer and broke cover. One time, the two of them had chased adventure, hopping a northbound train and taking it as far as Santa Cruz. She'd made it on board first and watched him running to catch the ladder on the side of the freight car as it picked up speed. They were both laughing and didn't stop until the kisses and sex took over. No laughs now, but she did watch him as he sprinted toward the coach. The Gatling rifle was loose and ready in his hand. Ammo packs were over his shoulder, as well as the TNT. His cavalry uniform was dusty and worn from the fight, but it only made him look more like a soldier, not a tin figure on parade.

And *Dios,* if he wasn't smiling when he made the final leap onto the side of the iron coach. He climbed up quickly and took up a position next to her.

"This circus keeps getting better and better." He fired at the flying Whisperer, who avoided his shots and sent two more down at them. Lead ricocheted off the metal top of the coach.

"Farrier's is almost gone."

He patted the satchel over his shoulder. "Still have some TNT. That'll stop the beast."

The towering machine still lumbered forward, reaching out with the sharp saw and grinding teeth.

"From the inside," she said. "We've got to blow it up from the guts out."

With a wink and a quick smile, he pulled a stick of dynamite from the satchel. "First we take care of the gunner below. Ready to jump?"

She collected herself, gripping the shotgun and slowing the coach to a sensible pace. He struck a match, cupped his hands around the flame and lit the fuse of the TNT. It was only going to be a short run to the mining machine. There were no Whisperers in their way.

He leaned down to toss the dynamite in the firing slot. "That wasn't a lie I told your parents. Meant every word."

"I know it." And she didn't hate him for it. Somewhere inside, she understood that he'd come back to Thornville because he would know to find her there. "And I know you're crazier than a spring coyote. Throw the damn dynamite."

The fuse was almost at its end. He stretched toward the firing slot. A black line slashed across his shoulder. Then came the crack of the shot from above. He lost his grip on the dynamite and it skipped away behind the coach. Baring his teeth in pain, he recoiled, gripping his arm.

She reached for him, but he held her off, gritting, "It ain't bad. It ain't bad."

A loud explosion sent a column of dirt and dust into the air behind them.

Rallying, he gathered himself. "That's our cover. Jump."

She burned with anger that he'd been hurt, but there was no time to check his injury. While the dust cloud was thinning, she and Tom leapt from the side of the rolling iron coach. The hard earth jarred her legs, and she fell to her hands and knees. Tom slid next to her. They grabbed each other to get upright again. Beneath his torn sleeve, a four-inch line of burned red flesh crossed his shoulder. But it didn't stop him. The two of them ran to the side of the mining machine.

The whole structure shook as it ate into the next building. The metal ladder on the side of the machine vibrated so hard, Rosa was almost thrown off. Tom was right behind, pressing against her on the ladder. Together they managed the ten-foot climb to the first hatch on the side. She yanked the latch, and he swung the door open.

Two shots from the flying Whisperer splintered into the wood next to them.

Tom growled, "Let's tear their heart out."

The two of them climbed through the hatch and into the massive mining machine.

Chapter Nine

LIKE A DINNER party in hell, the engines, cogs, and pistons were deafening. Quartz lights set high on the walls cast eerie yellow light on the inner workings of the mining machine. Huge gears turned, running chains and belts deep into other parts of the device.

Rosa and Tom stood on the landing of a winding staircase. She couldn't see into the darkness of the level beneath them, but above them, the machine gnashed and chattered.

Wincing, Tom checked the injury on his arm. "Sometimes an ether-charged bullet will burn the wound shut. No blood."

"Does it hurt?"

"Not as much as the thought of coming back and finding you married to Parker." It seemed like another wry jab, but his eyes were dead serious.

His depth nearly took her breath away. She said, "Then I guess you're well enough to keep fighting."

"Until the end."

Before she could answer, a dark shape below snagged her attention. Leading with his gun, a Whisperer charged up the stairs. Her trigger was quick. The soldier took the shot in the chest and tumbled back into the darkness.

She motioned Tom up on the stairs. "Looks like they're going to test your resolve."

His long legs spanned the steps in easy strides. "Gonna be an awful crowded boneyard."

Twisting up, the wooden staircase took them alongside the inner workings of the machine. Metal grinding wheels broke apart the shreds of buildings as they were drawn inward. The debris fell into sifting pans that shook back and forth. There was no gold and silver to be found here, only the remains of the citizens' hard work.

"Give me a couple of sticks of TNT."

Instead of getting them himself, he only turned so she had access to the satchel. While she retrieved them, he fired his Gatling rifle down the stairs, scattering more Whisperers coming for them. "Ain't going to be any more stairs left soon."

On the other side of the spinning gears and rattling chains, more Whisperers climbed a separate staircase.

"And no exits." With the dynamite in her hand, she searched for any option. The only hatch was two flights up, at the top of the fifty-foot machine.

He urged her up while firing at the Whisperers below.

"Don't know if you care to hear it, but there's something I gotta say."

The Whisperers ducked away from his shots and sent a couple of shotgun blasts up toward them. Wood splintered from a support beam five feet away.

"Before another word," she said, "you think you could hit those guys below us?"

"Can't yet. It's part of the plan."

"We don't have a plan."

"Sure we do." He spoke as if she'd been in on it all along. "Go for that high hatch."

They hurried past a rubberized belt looped around two gears powered by a howling tetrol engine. The machine's forward motion shook the whole structure. Close to the top, everything swayed like a ship on stormy seas.

One more set of stairs. Instead of being exposed to the inner workings of the device and the Whisperers on the other side of the open core, Tom and Rosa were protected by a large steel plate. The metal wall served as an anchor for several gears that spun, gnashing metal cogs against each other.

Tom caught Rosa's arm and slowed her down while they were still on the stairs, safe behind the metal wall.

"Hold up," he said. "This might be the last peace we know on this earth." He continued, an uncharacteristic depth in his eyes. "Been doing my talking with my guns, but it's not enough. You deserve the words. So what I got to say, Rosa, is that I'm sorry. For the way I left you. For not staying and fighting for you. Don't know if you want it, but there it is."

She did want it. The words didn't change the past, but they showed her something about the Tom who was with her now. Like finding an untarnished gold coin buried in the same dirt path she'd walked over a thousand times.

There was nowhere else to go. The top landing was just a few steps away. The wooden stairs bounced beneath their feet. All down the hollow center of the machine the gears and wheels turned. Whisperers were still on the opposite stairs and more were no doubt coming up this side toward them.

"It hurt like losing a limb then," she told Tom as he glanced up at the hatch in the wall at the top landing. "But we're both different now."

He absorbed her words, the emotions in his eyes deepening.

She continued, "I was trying to be something I wasn't." This would be easier to talk about over a bottle of tequila in Francis's saloon. "For my parents and the rest of the world. But not anymore. And you . . ." Danger bit down on them from all sides, like the teeth of a giant wolf. "You said you weren't the right man for me when you left. Damn right. But you are now. You've been with me every step of the way."

Tom double-checked his revolver and wound the rifle's clockwork. "Never want to leave you again."

"I think it had to be this way. We wouldn't have worked then. But now . . . we fit just right now."

He nodded as the understanding sank in. Bullets

didn't seem to matter for a moment. Their bodies could be hurt, but they lived in more than the flesh. She felt a fresh energy as what she already knew about herself was built up by Tom's strength.

The machine lurched all around them. More of the town poured into its voracious maw and was being ground to splinters. Tom sprinted up the last set of stairs, back into danger, and undid the latch on the hatch.

"You don't owe me any explanation. I'll take it, but you don't owe it. Why are you telling me this now?" he asked.

"Because I'm about to light the fuse." She pulled a match from her vest. It flared quickly with the acrid smell of sulfur. The fuses on the two sticks of dynamite caught fire and blazed.

Tom swung the hatch open. Sunlight streaked in, a solid shaft in the dusty air. She lobbed the TNT down the center of the machine and rushed for the exit with Tom.

"Ladder?" If only they could climb down faster than the fuses burned. She secured the rotary shotgun over her back.

"Not if the plan works." He slung the rifle on his shoulder and crouched at the exit. "Jump."

The sunlight was blinding, but she knew the fall would maim if not kill her. With Tom, though, she would leap into the unknown. They jumped together. Then she saw his plan. Hanging in the air outside the hatch was the Whisperer with the ether pack.

No way the soldier could've been expecting them to come busting out of the door. He didn't even have time to raise his pistol when the two of them slammed into him and latched on. Tom quickly chopped at the man's wrist with his hand, knocking the gun from his grip. The Whisperer tried to fight them off, but Tom punched him in the ribs, winding him.

"You see," Tom said with a wild grin, "if we'd killed all those Whisperers inside, they wouldn't have told this feller we were just on the other side of the hatch."

With the extra weight she and Tom added, the three of them quickly sank toward the ground. The buoyancy of the ether pack cushioned the descent, making it a hell of a lot better than falling straight down. But the fight wasn't over. The Whisperer continued to struggle, and someone was back in the driver's seat of the iron coach. The barrels of the Gatling gun looked like the black eyes of a tarantula as they swung around toward them.

"Gotta let go." Tom nodded toward the ground, then punched the Whisperer again in the gut.

They were still twelve feet off the ground. And the dynamite hadn't gone off yet. Maybe the machine destroyed the fuse before the spark had reached the explosive.

"Now," he urged her. "Right behind you."

Gravity tugged harder on her after she released her grip on the Whisperer. The hard earth was a jolt, and she rolled with the impact. Looking up, she saw Tom still struggling with the Whisperer. Damn it all, if she'd stayed up there she could have fought the man with him.

After throwing an angry-looking elbow into the soldier's head, Tom pulled back slightly and unholstered his pistol. Instead of aiming at the man, he put the barrel against one of the ether tanks. The shot pierced the metal. Tom let go and fell away as ether screamed out of the tank. The Whisperer streaked through the air, flailing his arms for control.

Tom hit the ground and stumbled forward until he caught his balance. He and Rosa watched the Whisperer slam into the side of the giant mining machine. Then the TNT exploded.

A concussive thump radiated across the ground. The Crandall device bucked and shuddered. A five-foot-round hole was blown out of the wood near the bottom. Flames licked across the wood. Broken gears screeched. Shattered metal clanged. The engines hissed, then rattled like a consumptive giving up their last breath. More fires blazed. With a loud pop, an engine blew. A gash opened up in the side of the machine and it started to buckle.

"There she goes!" Tom shouted excitedly. He ran to Rosa, and the two of them rushed through the street toward the canning building.

Behind them the machine's fuel and motors erupted. The blast separated her from Tom, knocking them both to the dirt. A huge grinding wheel tore out of the device and spun across the street. If she'd been standing, it would've cut her in half. Instead, the wheel whizzed above her and knocked a corner off the canning building, then lodged itself in a thick tree.

A few feet away, Tom recovered his hat from the ground. "Won't need to shave for a month."

More explosions wracked the halted mining machine. Wood splinters rained all over town. The saw blade clanged to a stop halfway into the telegraph office. Smoke rose from the ruined device, carrying the smell of burnt fuel and spring bonfires. The mining machine was dead.

A triumphant laugh bubbled up through her. She sprang to her feet, taking in the carcass of the Crandall device. "I told you not to come to Thornville," she said to the ruined machine.

Tom whooped behind her. Turning to him, her elation soared. It seemed like nothing could keep her from his arms. And from there, who knew?

But she didn't have a chance to find out. Instead, the iron coach came bouncing down the road behind her. A Whisperer leaned out of the open side door and hooked his arm around her waist. She was yanked from her feet. Her shotgun was torn from its sling and clattered in the dirt. Within an instant, she was carried away. As Tom streaked out of her vision, she saw three Whisperers rushing through the street toward him. Oh, God, there was nothing she could do to help him.

She jabbed backward into the Whisperer with her elbows. He hissed in pain when she contacted his ribs. With his grip loosened, she turned to face him and punched as hard as she could in the side of his neck.

The Whisperer's mask fell off as he stumbled backward into the bouncing coach. He tried to drag her with him. She pried at his clawing fingers. Her heart raced, thinking about Tom being outgunned.

"I've had enough of you bastards." Bracing her hands on the door frame, she kicked the man in the chest, sending him hard into the side of the mounted Gatling gun, then to the metal floor.

Her boots slipped on the edge of the coach as she tried to regain her footing. The ground was a rush of rocks and dirt below her. Trees blurred past. The coach sped down the road out of town, tetrol engine whining. Jumping would kill her.

From the look on the soldier's face and the muttered German curses, he wanted to kill her, too. Drawing her pistol was awkward as she teetered in the doorway. Her gun was halfway out when the man launched himself at her. She pulled the trigger but it was too late. The shot hit the ground as the man drove his shoulder into her chest.

Fingers like iron wrapped around her wrist. She and the soldier both slid precariously in the doorway. He continued growling in German as she tried to bring the gun around toward him.

She growled back. "Goddamn you. We beat you. Why don't you just die?"

It was time to end this fight. She stomped the heel of her boot into the top of his foot. He grunted, wincing, and slammed her hand against the metal side of the coach. Pain shot up her arm like red lightning. The pistol sprang from her grip and got caught up in the spinning rear wheel of the coach. She was jerked to the side as the gun was ripped from the lanyard.

Being off balance, she was the perfect target for the soldier. He shoved her body, trying to make her follow her pistol into the whirling iron wheel. She braced herself with one hand against the door frame. The other hand gripped the edge of the roof.

"I told you to die." Coiling her body, she brought her knee up hard into his jaw. The soldier's head snapped back, and he fell away into the coach.

Wind tugged at her. Nearby branches nearly whipped her off the side. She fought the bumpy ride and pulled herself up to the roof of the speeding iron coach. Behind her, Thornville shrank. The destroyed mining machine sent a column of smoke into the air, but it didn't feel like much of a victory anymore.

"Where the hell are you, Tom? You'd better be all right." He couldn't hear her hissed whisper, but maybe it would ride the wind toward town.

It felt like a giant bird of prey was swooping down on her. She turned toward the front of the coach just in time to see a thick tree branch quickly approaching. A hard dive took her to the roof and the branch swept over her.

Dry leaves clung to her hair and she brushed them out as she collected herself into a low crouch. The driver still hadn't noticed her. He wasn't one of the armored Whisperers, but he did wear an ether pistol on his hip. Her only chance was to get to him before he turned around. As soon as this fight was over, she promised herself, she would buy a nice two-shot derringer for her boot.

No time for hesitating. Every second took her further away from Tom and the fix he was in. She made one step toward the driver when the soldier from inside the coach hauled himself up on the roof with her. He wiped blood from the corner of his mouth with the back of his hand and sneered.

The driver finally turned and saw Rosa. His body stiffened with shock. He drew his pistol. One hand on the gun, the other on the steering lever, the driver split his attention between the path ahead and the fight she was about to get into with the very angry-looking soldier.

"Son of a bitch," Tom growled. Rosa was gone. Snatched away like a rabbit in the teeth of a mountain lion. A fast, iron-clad lion with metal-studded wheels. He'd never catch her on foot.

The Sky Charger should still be just on the other side of the canning building. He turned to run and bit down on another curse. Three Whisperers converged on him. There was no time to unsling his rifle.

"You ain't getting between me and Rosa." It didn't matter if they could hear him or understand his language. His revolver would tell the real story.

One Whisperer stopped running and twitched his gun toward Tom. The Rattler slid easily from its holster. He was faster than the Hapsburg soldier. From the hip, Tom pulled the secondary trigger and fired a shotgun shell.

The Whisperer fell. The remaining two didn't seem too eager to join him. They fanned out, hands poised over their ether pistols. Tom's pulse raced. How far was Rosa by now? How many men were in that coach? How many men was he going to have to kill to get to her?

These two Hapsburgs stood too far apart. He could get one, but the other would fire before he could swing his pistol around.

"I'll be damned if I'm going to wait for you two to decide which of you dies first."

He fired at the man on his left and dove forward, rolling onto the ground. The bullet creased the Whisperer's side. The man staggered, pawing at his gun but not able to pull it. But the other soldier did draw. His shot pierced where Tom had stood.

Tom came out of his roll firing. He shot a bullet and a shotgun blast into the second Whisperer. The soldier wasn't even on the ground when Tom turned on the other Hapsburg and emptied his last shotgun barrel into him.

Gunsmoke swirled around Tom as he sprinted toward the canning building. Behind it, Rosa's parents stood tensely with Whisperer shotguns in their hands.

Tom barked at them like they were shavetail privates. "You fuel it and water it?"

"*Sí,*" her father answered. "Yes. *Sí.*"

Her mother looked over Tom's shoulder with worried eyes. "Where is she?"

He couldn't answer. The words caught in his throat. There was no explaining, no time at all. All he knew was that he had to find her. He mounted the charger, bringing it into the air as he fired up the engine. As soon as the turbine turned, he kicked the lever for the fastest speed.

But the damn ether tank still struggled. The catalyst rattled like an old skeleton. As his velocity increased, the charger sank lower. It was agonizing, but he had to throttle back. Otherwise, he'd be digging a trench in the dirt trail, rather than skimming five feet above it.

"Come on. Come on. Get me to her." He leaned close to the charger's head, letting the wind whip around him. The machine had no ears, but it didn't matter. He even slapped the side of the metal neck with the reins.

The town was long behind him but there was no sign of the coach or Rosa on the road. A hill rose ahead of him. He sped up the side, only two feet off the ground. When he reached the top, he used the momentum to soar higher into the air.

Cold danger iced his back, replaced by the heat of purpose. He saw her. She stood on the top of the speeding coach. A tree branch rushed toward her and she dove to the roof just in time.

His muscles tensed, as if he was there with her, as if he could just reach out and lift her away to safety. But he was more than one hundred yards away.

Tom went into a dive on the charger, angling his descent so he'd catch the coach as it climbed the next hill. She had to hold on that long. She had to.

Rosa stalked toward the driver.

"That's right," Tom muttered between clenched teeth. "Get him. Throw that bastard from the top."

A soldier from inside the coach climbed onto the roof with her. Tom burned to go faster. If he could get his hands on that man, he'd crush the life out of him before he could touch Rosa. The danger escalated when the driver turned, seeing her and drawing his pistol.

Thirty yards. The Rattler was steady in Tom's hand,

but it was too far a shot for the short barrel. If he missed the Hapsburgs, he could hit Rosa.

The soldier on top with her launched into an attack. Tom always knew she was the devil of a woman. This day had proved that. She had fought with enough determination to stop a three- story mining machine. And now he got to witness her bring a living hell to the man in front of her.

While the man swung his fists wildly, she sneered and kicked him on the inside of his knee. He buckled. She followed up with a hard punch to his face. It wasn't enough to knock him out. The soldier pushed forward and tackled her onto the roof.

Tom's gut clenched. Twenty yards. Ten. Rosa rolled with the soldier. The son of a bitch tried to throw her from the roof, but she shifted her weight, taking them back to the middle.

More speed meant less height, so Tom could only fly closer in agonizing increments. He was coming along the right side of the speeding coach when three shots rang out. The driver had spotted him.

Weaving in the air, Tom felt the shots burn past. He also felt Rosa's eyes on him. She and the soldier had frozen their fight for a moment. Great relief showed in her face, and Tom felt he could fly to her even without the charger. There was nothing sentimental in the look from the soldier. Pure hate.

Tom shared the emotion.

The driver seemed to hesitate, trying to figure out whether Rosa or Tom should be his next target. Tom wasn't going to let him make the decision. Two quick shots from the Rattler found their mark in the driver's body. The man pitched forward, firing his own gun into the coach's controls. Metal shattered and ground—the sickly sounds of a machine that wasn't going to work right anymore.

Bellowing in outrage, the soldier redoubled his efforts to throw Rosa from the roof. The path was straight for a while ahead of the coach, but with a dead driver slumped over the controls, any hazard on the road would be a disaster for Rosa.

She fought the soldier off, kicking him in the gut and the hip until the two of them separated. They got to their feet and circled, too close for Tom to get off a shot.

He called to her, only about ten feet from the side of the coach. "Ain't got time for you to be dancing with another man."

"I'd rather be dancing with you."

The soldier split his attention between Rosa and Tom. He bled from his lip, his eyebrow. Didn't look like he wanted to take another beating from Rosa. Instead he slid to the side of the coach and swung down through the open side door.

Rosa rushed to the controls, pushing the driver aside to take his seat. But nothing worked. She jammed the pedals and levers, and still the coach bounced at a breakneck pace along the path.

"He shot the controls," Tom explained.

"Well how the hell am I . . . ?"

He extended his hand toward her from the charger. They were only about eight feet apart.

"Jump it."

She shook her head. "Fly up here and get me."

"No lift. Keeping this pace, this is as high as I get."

Movement inside the coach tightened his clock springs. The soldier shifted the Gatling gun's mount. The barrels receded from the front firing slot. Holy hell, he could aim the gun out the side door, right at Tom.

And then Rosa would die, too. Either falling off the coach or crushed in a terrible wreck.

He waved her toward him with one hand, forcing the words out as he felt the tension like a noose. "Rosa. Rosa, I love you."

She stood stunned. "Why are you telling me that now?"

The stick of dynamite in his other hand was the answer. He pulled a match from a pouch on his belt and lit the fuse.

Two quick steps took her to the edge of the coach, then she leapt. Tom caught her with one arm. She wrapped herself around him. It felt like he took the first breath of his life, having her back with him.

She eyed the lit dynamite in his hand. "A romantic man would've brought flowers."

"Well he ain't gonna start shooting chocolate bonbons at us."

The nose of the Gatling gun poked out of the side door. Tom swung the charger close for a second and tossed the TNT into the coach. Rosa tightened her grip on him and he yanked on the reins. As the charger slowed, the coach sped away.

A flash of light burst within the iron coach. The metal bulged and split, pushed out by the explosion. The wheels sprang free and sped ahead as the twisted body of the coach tumbled forward in a rooster tail of smoke and fire. A final screech and the iron carcass came to a stop, smoldering on the dirt trail.

Tom brought the charger to rest on the ground, and he and Rosa dismounted to catch their breath. A fresh quiet surrounded them. No gunshots or explosions. Just the wind in the oak leaves.

And Rosa in his arms to tell him the world was still worth living in. He gripped her tight, and she did the same. They were both battered from the fight. A bruise darkened the corner of her cheek. Hot iron seared at his shoulder, and he remembered that he'd been grazed there by an ether bullet.

But hell if all that didn't matter.

She gave his hip a little shove. "You owe me a bottle of good tequila. I got more soldiers than you did."

"I got more. And I want my bottle of applejack."

"How about we buy each other a bottle and call it even?"

"That's a deal."

Sunlight showed all the rich brown of her eyes. Their depth was unimaginable. He wanted to dive in. Her mouth moved, but she didn't speak. A little smile, and then she did speak.

"I love you, too."

More than any ether tank, more than any modern invention, he was lifted up by the words and the strength of this woman before him. "But we're out of dynamite."

The kiss drew him tighter to her. He felt every pulse of his blood through his body, and every place where she was pressed close. They pulled apart and stood holding each other. He unwound his hands from her and tugged at the hammered shell casing around his left ring finger. It slipped over his knuckles, and he didn't miss it. The ring clinked dully into one of the leather pouches on his belt.

She kissed him again, quick, then licked her lips like a hungry predator. "There's plenty of dynamite."

Chapter Ten

THE HONEST SOUND of hammer against nails rang through Thornville. Fresh-cut wood smelled like progress and healing. With Parker as gang boss, the half-eaten telegraph office had been finished in record time. Now every able body worked on repairing the blacksmith's and farrier's buildings. The stable could wait, and a temporary corral held the horses, who watched the work with passing interest.

Rosa stood in the middle of the street, watching the town come back to life. Behind her, the corner of the canning building that had been damaged was getting a new coat of paint. The blackened wood of the mining machine had been cleared out as soon as it had stopped burning. But there were still genuine Crandall men sifting through the area for anything salvageable.

They cast furtive glances at Rosa, gun-shy of approaching lest they got another tongue-lashing like the one she gave them when they'd first shown up. Idiot corporate men who couldn't keep their equipment properly guarded during a war. They insisted it would never happen again. Tom explained that if it did, every Crandall man would be considered a traitor to his country and dealt with appropriately. Looking from the stripes on his uniform to the star on her vest, the mining men shrank away.

And then Tom had to go away. It hadn't even taken twenty-four hours after he'd returned as a soldier for him to make himself indispensable in her life. Not just in the battle with the Hapsburg saboteurs. But he fit just right next to her. They'd both grown to the point where they complemented each other's strengths. She could never question his loyalty again. His dedication to her was like a campfire and a blanket over her shoulders on a cold night. And a Winchester across her lap.

The chill had crept into her nights after he left this time. It was only a couple of days after the fight with the Hapsburgs, shorter than his leave should've been. But he said the Army had to know. The enemy might try the same thing somewhere else. This was no excuse to run. She saw in his eyes how much he wanted to stay. He didn't sneak away like before. Instead, he flew boldly off on his Sky Charger in broad daylight.

A shadow skimmed along the ground, and she shaded her eyes to look in the sky. Tom rode down from forty feet above her, relaxed in the saddle and looking crisp in a new uniform. But she knew polished buttons and a stripe down the side of his thigh couldn't completely tame him.

Dios, his wild side was all hers. His arrival breathed new life into her. It felt like she could soar into the air to meet him twenty feet over the ground.

"Howdy, Sheriff," he called down, pinching his brim, a wicked little smile on his face.

"Sergeant."

Shaking his head, he pointed to the new patches on his shoulder. "Second Lieutenant."

As he flew closer the smell of roasting carrots reminded her of when they flew back to Thornville after her wild iron coach ride. It seemed then as if her heart would never stop pounding. But that might've been Tom's doing, not the crashing death she'd avoided.

Coming in high, they had seen the burning ruin of the mining machine and the splintered remains of the buildings it had destroyed. Her parents and some others had surrounded the surviving Hapsburg soldiers, containing them with their own guns. Parker had saddled the fastest horse to ride to the closest authorities.

Once the fires had been put out and the soldiers had been tied up and secured in a barn, she and Tom had walked together to Francis's saloon. The bottle of tequila was on the house.

She was brought back to the present as Tom landed near her and dismounted, stretching his legs. He untied his saddlebags and slung them over his shoulder. But as he walked toward her, a new worry tightened her ribs.

"A promotion," she said. "Does that mean they're giving you a platoon of men to command at the front?"

"Nope." He took off his hat and ran his hand through

his short blond hair. "It means they're giving me a territory."

The smile grew on his face. Bold in broad daylight, he wound his arms around her waist. No doubt the town was watching. Including her parents. Rosa was the sheriff. She did what she wanted.

She kissed Tom, and he kissed her back.

When they pulled apart, he indicated a small metal insignia pinned on his collar. "You're looking at the very first Upland Ranger in the Home Guard division. Top brass started it up on my recommendation." He gazed over the town and the hills that surrounded it. "It's my duty to keep the home front safe from any more enemy attacks. And . . ." His hand gripped hers. "I get to work closely with local authorities in my territory."

She hoped the top brass knew what was good for them. "Which includes Thornville."

"Bet your ass it does. I made sure of that. No way I'm fighting the enemies of our country without you at my side."

It sounded right, the two of them protecting the land. "They have you barracked in San Luis?" They started walking down the street, toward her sheriff's office.

"I'm a platoon of one. Barracked wherever I hang my pistol." He still held her hand. "Was hoping there might be a place for me in Thornville."

"There's a little house that'll be perfect for you. It's got only one other resident."

"But she's a wildcat."

"As untamed as you."

"Sounds all right by me." He took his eyes from her to glance up the street. "What'll *they* think about it?"

Her parents stood in front of their leather shop, watching Tom and Rosa's approach. But she didn't feel any hesitation in his step. He stood tall and close to her.

"They haven't stopped talking about how you came back a mighty fine *hombre*."

"We'll all have to sit down for a talk sometime soon. Some serious matters to work out."

With Tom, it didn't sound like shackles. He wanted her for who she was. Being with him was freedom.

"I'll make sure there's plenty of tequila."

"Still haven't had my applejack."

It was true. After the fight, they went straight from the saloon to her house. To sleep. To make love. To eat and make love again until he had to leave.

"I'm buying," she said.

He hesitated and she pulled out of his hand.

"Brought you a gift." He rummaged in his saddlebag and handed her a small cardboard box.

It was heavy. "Jewelry?"

"Well, it is pretty."

The box slid open, revealing a gleaming two-barrel derringer.

He watched her face. "But not as pretty as you. Or as dangerous."

"The perfect accessory for any fancy lady." Heat flushed over her skin. Not only did he know her body, but he understood her deeper than anyone else. "Better than any jewelry."

There was a surprising gravity in his eyes. "You already knew I'm not a romantic man."

"You're a lot of things." She took all of him in, amazed that he was real and complete in front of her. "But you're not the Tom who left."

"Hell no. And you ain't the Rosa who stayed."

"Good thing." She tucked the derringer into the top of her boot and pulled him into another kiss. "Everything fell into place."

"Like the cylinder turning to a fresh chamber as the hammer falls."

They kissed again, their bodies pressed close. Her star clinked against one of his brass buttons. "If I was still the old me," she said, "I wouldn't have been ready for who you are now."

"I'm yours." She felt the ferocious truth in his words. "Soldier, roughneck, hell of a dancer, lover, straight shot."

All of that and more.

"You're the man who came back."

If you loved NIGHT OF FIRE
don't miss novellas from Zoë Archer,
the other half of the smart, sexy
Ether Chronicles collaboration

SKIES OF FIRE

Man-made of metal and flesh

Captain Christopher Redmond has just one weakness: the alluring spy who loved and left him years before . . . when he was still just a man. Now superhuman, a Man O' War, made as part of the British Navy's weapons program, his responsibility is to protect the skies of Europe. If only he could forget Louisa Shaw.

A most inconvenient desire

Louisa, a British naval intelligence agent, has never left a job undone. But when her assignment is compromised, the one man who can help her complete her mission is also the only man ever to tempt her body and heart. As burning skies loom and passion ignites,

Louisa and Christopher must slip behind enemy lines if they are to deliver a devastating strike against their foe . . . and still get out alive.

Available Now
Wherever E-books Are Sold

Coming in October 2012

Daphne Carlisle must journey into
perilous territory to free her parents
from a warlord's clutches.
Her only hope of reaching them is Captain
Mikhail Denisov, a rogue Man O' War
as seductive as he is untrustworthy.
Yet she needs Mikhail and the airship he both
commands and powers through the technological
enhancements implanted in his body.
Mikhail thinks he has the mission
and Daphne figured out:
a simple job and a beautiful, sheltered woman.
But this jaded mercenary is about to learn
that in the world of the Ether Chronicles,
appearances can be deceptive.

About the Author

NICO ROSSO was a writer in search of a genre until his wife, Zoë Archer, brought romance into his life in more ways than one. Through her he learned the romance genre was filled with vast opportunities for storytelling. He created the sci-fi romance Limit War series, sweeping readers off Earth to an interstellar conflict. Closer to home, he set off the apocalypse with *The Last Night*. And starting with The Ether Chronicles, he gets to write closer than ever with his wife. They created the steampunk world together and trade off telling romance tales that span the globe. You can find him on the web at www.nicorosso.com.

Give in to your impulses . . .
Read on for a sneak peek at four brand-new e-book original tales of romance from Avon Books.
Available now wherever e-books are sold.

An Excerpt from

CIRCLE OF DANGER

by Carla Swafford

The top-secret assassins of The Circle are back and on the hunt for a dangerous drug lord capable of bringing women to the brink of pleasure . . . and devastation.

Marie Beltane, a lowly data-entry specialist intent on proving she's worthy of being a full operative, has just been injected with the drug responsible for the death of four local women . . . a drug that puts her sex drive into overdrive.

Arthur Ryker wants nothing more than to protect Marie, even if it means fulfilling her drug-induced . . . needs. But now a new evil has reared its ugly head—how far is Arthur willing to go to find an antidote and save the woman he always loved?

AN AVON RED NOVEL

CHAPTER ONE

Arthur Ryker sprang out of bed and immediately stood at attention, feet apart, his scarred hands in the "ready" position at waist level. One hand cupped by the other, restrained but prepared to kill. He shook his head and sighed. Just once he wanted to leave his bed like a regular person and not like a trained monkey.

"A bad dream?" a deep voice asked from the bedroom entrance. With one pierced black eyebrow lifted, Jack Drago leaned against the doorjamb.

Ignoring the question, Ryker walked naked into the bathroom. When he returned to grab some clothes out of the closet, Jack hadn't moved, but his gaze had most likely inspected every inch of the room. There wasn't much to see. A king-sized bed sat in a corner while a mirrorless dresser was centered against one wall—no pictures or the usual bric-a-brac to give away the occupant's personality. Then again, maybe it did. Rather stark for a man who owned enough properties and businesses to keep his organization in the best covert weapons money could buy. He didn't care what Jack thought about his bedroom. Except for a few hours of sleep and a shower and shave, Ryker rarely spent time in the room.

"What do you want?" he asked, glaring at his second-in-command.

With cold blue eyes, Jack studied him, then his gaze shifted away.

Ryker grunted. Not many people could deal with looking at the thick scars down the side of his body, but it was his blind eye that bothered most. White from the scar tissue damaged in a fire so many years ago, it was normally hidden beneath a patch. But Ryker'd be damned before he slept with one on. So if Jack decided to make a habit of waking him in the morning, he could fucking well get use to the sight. Considering the man had four visible piercings—and who knew how many hidden—along with tattoos covering one arm, Jack shouldn't have a problem with his scars. The man understood pain.

With sure, quick movements, he thrust his legs into jeans and yanked on a black T-shirt. After tugging on his boots, he strapped a small pistol at his ankle. With his patch in place, using his fingers he combed hair over the strap securing its position. Hell, he needed a haircut again. Maybe he'd shave his head like Jack. A simple enough solution. If only the rest of his problems could be so easily solved.

"She's in trouble," Jack said in an even tone as if his voice could defuse a bad situation.

Ryker's stomach and chest tightened as if he'd been hit. He knew who Jack referred to without adding a name. She happened to be part of why his life was so complicated.

"Did you hear me?" Jack straightened his stance.

"Yeah." Desire to break someone's neck raced through his body. "Where is she? What happened?"

With a sharp snap, he inserted a snub-nose into the shoulder holster hanging at his side and jerked on his leather jacket. He gritted his teeth for a few seconds to regain his composure. Then he took a deep breath, squared his shoulders, and exhaled.

"Last time Bryan heard from her, she'd entered the target's house in Chattanooga and was downloading information off a laptop. He lost communication with her." Jack quickly stepped out of the way for Ryker to move into the dark hallway. "They believe she's still in the house. If the Wizard sticks to his MO, we'll have about three hours before he takes her away or kills her."

Ryker wasted no time in reaching a massive room with mirrors from ceiling to floor. When the mansion was built in the eighteen hundreds, the room was used as a ballroom. It was empty now, except for a Steinway covered with a white sheet, and the high-sheen hardwood floor sounded hollow as he tramped across it. He used the room for one purpose only—to reach the stairwell hidden behind one of the mirrors.

"Took you long enough to spit it out." Ryker glanced at his second-in-command.

Jack remained quiet, staring straight ahead. Ryker didn't really expect an excuse. The man knew how he felt about that. No excuse for failure, especially when it came to protecting Marie.

Four months earlier, Ryker had moved The Circle compound from the suburbs of Atlanta to an area near the Smoky

Mountains. The mansion was situated in the middle of almost ten thousand acres, which included a large mountain filled with a network of tunnels and bunkers perfect to house the facility he needed. Last year, the final phase of the project was completed and now they were training new recruits in the underground Sector. The nearly fifteen square miles provided the privacy he needed. In a world filled with evil people, his covert organization of assassins came in handy.

Their footsteps echoed in the long, well-lit tunnel. A semi could pass through the passageway without scraping the side mirrors or the tips of muffler stacks.

"Who was her backup?" Ryker asked.

When a few seconds passed without an answer, Ryker stopped and faced Jack.

"They're handling it."

Ryker continued to stare.

His second-in-command sighed. "She went in without a backup."

Jaw clenched, Ryker strode to the iris scan next to a large metal door. A buzz sounded and he slammed the door against the inner wall.

The gripping pain in his belly grew and reminded him of the fear he had lived with for years before he took over control of The Circle. She could not keep doing this to him. He refused to allow anything more to happen to her. She knew this and still didn't listen.

The noise level in the basketball court-sized room almost broke the sound barrier with printers running and people shouting or talking to those sitting next to them—or to others on the Internet or satellite phones—along with the clicking of keyboards. Each wall covered with large screens captured a different scene of people living their lives in various parts of the world. In the center of the room, faces bleached white by the monitors in front of them, the supervisors and handlers communicated with their operatives.

Ryker stopped in the middle of the bullpen, searching for his prey.

The balding, whipcord-thin Bryan Tilton stood over a handler shouting instructions and pointing at the screen. Maybe a sixth sense alerted Bryan. He looked up and his eyes widened.

Ryker charged toward him, ignoring the people ducking for cover behind partitions and beneath desks.

"You son of a bitch!"

His fist clipped Bryan on the chin, sending the man sliding across the floor. Desire to flatten the asshole's pointy nose almost overrode all of Ryker's control. Good thing Bryan remained sprawled out on the linoleum.

Standing over the man, Ryker opened and closed his fists. The temptation to punish him further for his stupidity warred with the fear of jabbing the cartilage of the idiot's nose into his brain.

"I swear, sir, I told her to wait until I could get backup in place, but she wouldn't listen." Bryan cupped his jaw and shifted it from side to side. "Two of our operatives are held up in a traffic accident about twenty-five miles from her last location."

"Last location?" Ryker gritted his teeth.

"The target's house, off Riverview Road." Bryan scooted back when Ryker took a step. The man's head bobbled on his skinny neck. "As soon as Phil and Harry reach it, they'll extract her."

Afraid he would crack the man's chicken neck, Ryker turned away and pointed at the nearest handler. "You! Sal?"

Mohawk trembling, the pale man nodded.

Ryker said, "Tell Phil and Harry to call me on my cell as soon as they reach the house. Do not go inside! Jack and I will be there in twenty minutes. Have them wait for us. AHH" He turned back to Bryan. "Have the Spirit ready in five minutes." His helicopter could cover the miles quickly and land almost anywhere.

Marie Beltane struggled against the chains restraining her on a cot that reeked of sex and urine. She stifled a groan. No, no, no. Nausea traveled up her throat.

All the beams and pipes overhead felt like they were squeezing the air out of the room. Basements were never among her favorite rooms. The dampness and creepy-crawly things always gave her the willies.

She still couldn't believe she'd been caught. Bryan had sworn it would be an easy gig. Prior surveillance had revealed the man worked each evening at a massive bank of computers. Go in and download a flash drive load of info and get out. The target always left his house at nine in the morning and didn't return until nine that evening. Breaking into the house when most people ate dinner in the surrounding homes had sounded so easy. Few would look out their windows as they settled down in front of their plates or televisions or both.

Hours would pass before he returned home. But he came back early.

Oh, God, she'd screwed up big time!

He looked like a fourteen-year-old with his cartoon-themed T-shirt and his mop of hair, but she knew from his file he was between twenty-six and twenty-eight. During their surveillance, they never got a clear photograph of him. Whenever he entered or exited his house, he did so through his garage. His SUV had tinted windows, preventing anyone from seeing inside.

The man standing with his back to her had outmaneuvered every defensive tactic she'd been taught. He didn't fight like a kid. Jack was right. She needed to work harder on her moves. If she had, she wouldn't be in this predicament. The nerd had surprised her, taking her down with unexpected ease.

She refused to cry even though she couldn't stop the trembling in her body. Every inch ached from his battery of hits and kicks. For a scrawny man, he'd moved fast and hit hard.

Her head hurt from holding back tears. She'd hoped never to be in this position again, to be under someone's control. No matter how many times she reminded herself this was different from before, the horror of repeating history pushed her to keep her eyes open. Staying aware of her enemy helped to keep her calm.

"You're not very smart. I'm efficient in seven different types of martial arts." His stiff words failed to impress her. He moved, revealing what he held in his hand. The huge syringe with a shiny green substance in the barrel had a needle longer than her forefinger. "Just because I'm a geek doesn't mean I'm unacquainted with ways to defend myself."

Marie stared at the needle. The duct tape covering her mouth muffled her scream. Ever since he jumped her, she'd tried to see a way to escape, while keeping calm.

She tried to be brave. She kept telling herself that screaming would only be a waste of energy. Stifling the panic engulfing her would keep her alive.

"Wait until this stuff hits your bloodstream. I'm told the sensation is similar to that last second before reaching an orgasm. In other words, you'll do anything to get off." He chuckled and lifted her shirt. He tugged at the waistband of her jeans.

She flinched when the needle slid into the soft skin near her hip.

"Perfect for where I'm sending you." He jerked on the jeans until the tips of his fingers brushed her pubic hair. "White American women—especially petite, natural blondes like you—are quite popular in parts of the Middle East and Asia. Virgins are preferred but rare here unless we go much younger." He shrugged. "Then you get into Amber Alerts and they're too much trouble. Anyway, bitches like you are plentiful and disposable."

He pulled harder at her jeans, taking her panties down.

She froze. Her stomached churned with the thought of what he might do next. Then he pushed the needle deeper. The liquid burned, becoming hotter as he eased the plunger down. The pain took her mind off her fear for only a second. When she tried to move away, the rattling chains reminded her she wasn't going anywhere. Tears pooled at the corner of her eyes and she turned her head, refusing to let him see her cry.

"A formula created by . . . a fucking genius! Especially created to use on sneaky sluts like you. The Wizard is a god!" He laughed. The back of his hand grazed her cheek. "I know it stings, baby. Sorry . . . no. I'm not sorry. You have the look of an ice princess. I love seeing an uptight cunt like you suffer. You have no idea what you've gotten yourself into. This wonder drug is highly addictive and from what I'm told, it has long-lasting effects. You'll grow to love it."

The grin on his smooth face terrified her more than anything else he'd done. Her vision blurred. The man leaned over her, his brown eyes dark and merciless. She whimpered. Every cell of her body tingled.

"Do you feel it? It takes a little while to set in. The Wizard said it tingles all over and next, for a small time, you'll feel like you're floating on water. Then you'll get sleepy and then—*bam!*—you'll be like a bitch in heat." He cackled and thrust his groin several times against her leg and the side of the cot. He punched the air with his fist and did a little dance. When he turned his back, he reached for something on a table nearby. "Now let's see what all of you looks like."

Light glinted off the scalpel. He swiped at the air above her as if he wielded a sword. No matter how brave she tried to be earlier, she couldn't stop her limbs from shaking harder and her stomach from twisting. She squealed behind the tape.

The sound of slicing material had her arching away from his touch. *Please don't cut me. Oh, please, God, help.* In seconds, he peeled away her clothes. He rubbed his groin and a lascivious grin marred his youthful face.

"Not bad, though I find the scars a shame, yet rather interesting. It looks like someone used a belt or whip on you.

Have you been a bad girl?" He slid his hand down her bare thigh and over a long, thin white scar. "There are clients who would love to add to them."

She turned her head. Swallowing several times to keep from choking on vomit, she concentrated on the number of blocks in the basement wall. She could get through this. It wouldn't be the first time her body had been used. Eventually, she'd find a way out.

Just as she heard his zipper go down, a loud blast shook the walls. Dust sprinkled onto her face. She blinked her eyes. The room looked smoky, choked with plaster powder.

"What the hell?" The man ran toward the stairs as he struggled to pull up his pants. One foot on the bottom step, he stopped, staring at the door.

A smaller blast was followed by shouting and heavy footsteps running across the floor above. Whoever had come a-knocking were making their way through the house.

"Well, babe, you're on your own. I hope they appreciate the gift I'm leaving them." He laughed and disappeared beneath the stairs into a black void.

Her eyelids felt so heavy. Tingling traveling across her torso rushed down her legs and arms, and then a feeling of lightness and floating followed. A strong breeze brushed her naked body. Someone had found the basement. A wave of dizziness pushed her under and she closed her eyes, unable to lift them even when she felt someone fighting with the chains holding her down.

"Damn it, Marie. You'd better be alive," a deep voice growled.

She smiled. Deep inside, she knew he'd come for her.

An Excerpt from

HEAT RISES

by Alice Gaines

Welcome to Alice Gaines's "Cabin Fever" series: Who knows what naughty games you'll play when you've got nowhere else to go? Laura Barber gets to put her imagination to the test when she finds herself snowbound in a cabin with Ethan Gould, a man she's dreamt of doing unspeakably delicious things to for years. Find out what happens when . . . *Heat Rises.*

AN AVON RED NOVELLA

CHAPTER ONE

So much for making it to her job interview. Laura Barber might as well have been looking at a moonscape rather than a deserted mountain highway. Still shivering, she gazed out the window of the country store as the falling snow covered the pavement and filled in the road completely. The storm had started only half an hour ago. What would this place look like by morning?

"You're a mighty lucky young lady," said the shopkeeper, handing her a Styrofoam cup with steam coming out the top. "If you'd gone off the road any farther from here, you'd still be out in that."

She took a sip of the coffee and did her best not to grimace at the bitter taste. The man may be right about her luck, but she'd probably ruined her shoes on the trek here. The low-heeled pumps had cost a bundle, and she'd worn them just enough that her feet felt comfortable when she dressed for business.

"Yep," the man said as he gazed out at the accumulating snow. "Nobody'll be moving around in these parts for days."

"Mister—"

"Beaumont," he said, offering his gnarled hand.

"Mr. Beaumont," she said, studying him as they shook hands. The twinkle in his blue eyes suggested more youth than the fringe of white hair did. If you called central casting for a country store owner, they'd probably send someone like this man.

"You'd be in a heap of trouble if you'd broken down farther away," he said.

"Can someone come out and put me back on the road before things get worse?" she asked.

"You don't understand storms in these mountains, Miss."

"Ms.," she said. "Ms. Laura Barber."

"Well, Ms. Barber, won't nobody get out of here until the plows come through."

"When will that be?"

"Days," he answered. "Probably not a week, though."

"A week?" Darn it all. She was supposed to be at the bottom of this mountain by evening and at an interview in the morning. She'd planned carefully to get ahead of this storm, but her plane had landed late. Still, she ought to have been able to make her destination. She'd grown up in Connecticut and had driven in winter weather before. Snow was snow, wasn't it? Apparently not.

"What am I going to do?" she asked. "I can't stay here for days."

"That you can't. I'll be closing up and heading home in a few minutes."

"Is there a motel nearby?" she asked.

"Nope. We'll have to find a family to put you up."

"I can't impose on strangers for days."

He shrugged. "Don't see that you have much choice."

Wonderful. Not only would she not make it to her interview but she'd also have to spend days with people she didn't know. She managed well enough in business situations where procedures and rules of engagement were clearly laid out. In someone's home, she'd have to interact. She probably couldn't disappear behind her laptop without appearing rude.

"Unless . . ." Mr. Beaumont said. "Your solution might be pulling up right now."

Headlights shone in from outside—bright enough to blind her for a moment—a huge SUV or pickup, with its engine at a low roar. The motor shut off, and the lights went dim. A man climbed out and headed into the store. A blast of cold air whooshed in through the front as he entered. "Hey, Phil."

Mr. Beaumont shuffled off. "Hey, you young pup. What are you doing out in weather like this?"

"Business down in the city. Thought I could outrun the storm."

The voice tugged at her memory. Low and dark. She knew it. Even though she hadn't heard it recently enough to place it in her brain, something about the tone registered in her body.

She glanced over at the counter where he stood, his back to her. Tall and broad-shouldered, he commanded the space around him. She had a physical memory of that too, enough to warm her skin. Whoever this was, she'd do best to avoid him. But how?

"Good thing you're here," Mr. Beaumont said, gesturing toward her. "This lady is going to need a ride somewhere."

The man turned and all the memory nudges turned into one huge sucker punch. Ethan Gould.

Good Lord, not him. It had to be five years . . . no, six. That night at the party. After three years of fantasies about the handsome guy who always sat at the front of the class, she'd decided to at least try to find out if the attraction was mutual. Tequila fortification, too much, had led to a night of humiliation. Oh God, all the things she'd said to him. Her stomach sank remembering them after all this time.

Other than that, they'd almost never interacted all through business school. He'd have forgotten her by now. Women probably came on to him all the time—women more remarkable than herself. He wouldn't remember. Please God, don't let him remember.

Sure enough, he smiled at her as he would at any stranger. A genial expression he used so easily. The famed Gould charm would come next. So potent it worked even on men. On women . . . well, forget trying to resist it.

After a moment, his brows knitted together. "Do we know each other?"

"No . . . I don't think . . . haven't met," she said. Damn it all, how could he force this reaction from her after so much time? She'd actually lie about her identity if she could get away with it. She'd avoided him successfully since that horrible night. She'd actually followed his career so that she'd know where he was. He couldn't have just happened on her on a snowy mountain, and yet here he stood, as tempting and as terrifying as he'd been at that party.

"This is Ms. Laura Barber," Mr. Beaumont said. "You two know each other?"

"Right." Recognition dawned in his amber eyes, followed by a slight tension to his jaw. Remembering, no doubt. Her skin went from warm to burning. By now, her face would be a bright pink.

He recovered quickly, with a big smile. He still had perfect teeth, of course, and perfect skin. Only his too-large ears kept him from total perfection, but the flaw made him all the more attractive.

"It's been a while," he said. "Good to see you again."

"Hi." A stupid reply but innocent enough, she thought.

"Seeing as you two know each other, won't you mind taking Ms. Barber to where she wants to go?" Mr. Beaumont asked.

He rested a hand on a nearby rack of magazines and struck a casual pose. A light of cunning in his eyes belied his apparent ease. "Where are you headed?"

"The city," she said. "I'm already late."

"How'd you get this far?"

"Rental car"—she gestured toward the outside as if she could point at the thing—"I ran off the road."

"Can't say I'm surprised," he said, his gaze never leaving her face. She did her best to look straight back at him, but she'd never win a staring contest with this man. Eventually, she gave up and studied his shoes, instead. Boots, rather—the sort ranchers wore. His had a broken-in appearance, as did the faded jeans that covered his legs up to the hem of his shearling jacket.

"We won't be getting to the city tonight," he said. "But we can make it to my friend's cabin."

"Cabin?" she repeated. "In the middle of a blizzard?"

"My friend's an engineer. The place is self-sufficient with a generator and solar panels."

"The sun's not out now," she said. In fact, with the heavy snow, it was already dark.

"And storage batteries," he said. "We'll be fine."

"I haven't agreed to go with you."

"What choice do you have?" he asked, as he straightened and pulled a slip of paper from his jacket. "I'll need a few things, Phil."

"Coming right up." Mr. Beaumont took the list from him and retreated to the back of the store.

"Look, this is really nice of you—"

Before she could get the "but" out, he took a step toward her. " 'Nice' isn't exactly the word I was thinking of."

She made herself stand her ground, even though everything in her wanted to back away. "I don't want to impose."

"Don't be silly. No one around here would put someone out on a night like this."

"Mr. Beaumont said he'd find a family here to take me in."

He crossed his arms over his chest. "So, you're a social butterfly now? Happy to move in with strangers for several days?"

Damn him, he knew she wasn't. He had to remember from graduate school that she kept to herself, quietly getting top grades from her place in the back of the class.

"I . . . I . . ." Damn it. He actually had her stuttering. She took a breath. "I can't go with you."

"Why not?" he asked, as he studied her, his gaze assessing and not without a light of admiration. Her heartbeat responded, speeding up. The feeling might be pleasant with another man—one who hadn't heard about her sexual fantasies after she'd had too many margaritas. She'd told him about how her mind had wandered during boring lectures, imagining how his hands would feel on her breasts. About how she played images of him in her mind when she used her vibrator. She'd even asked if his sex was as big as she'd imagined it, and then giggled when she'd fumbled against his pants and discovered it was even larger. Oh God, humiliation. Utter and total humiliation.

"Maybe you're afraid to be alone with me," he said. He might have read her mind.

"Ridiculous." Okay, that was a lie, but she wouldn't cower before him. She'd gone on from that night to establish a good career. As a grown woman with more experience since graduate school, she shouldn't have to fear men any longer, even this one. Even if she did, she wouldn't let him know he frightened her.

"Laura, you have a choice of crowding in with a family you don't know or sharing a cabin with me. I won't even speak to you if you don't want."

"I don't think that will be necessary." Great. She'd agreed to go with him. No matter. A few days together, and she'd get away again.

"Good." He smiled yet again, the blasted man. "The cabin it is."

You could have knocked Ethan Gould over with a feather. First, to run into Laura Barber at Phil Beaumont's store, way out here in the middle of no place. At least there was a logical explanation for that. She was probably up for the same job at Henderson that he was. A bit odd, as their talents—skill sets, she would have called them—lay in very different areas. But they were both übercompetent, as any headhunter would have to know. Still, what were the chances that she'd end up at that country store, needing a ride in one of the mountains' worst storms of the season just as he pulled in? Fate was trying to tell them something, and he, for one, was listening.

The fact that she'd end up staying with him in an isolated cabin fell into a different category of unlikelihood. Impossibility, more like. And yet, there she sat in the bucket seat next to his, staring out at the snow as if it held some message.

Laura Barber, the shy thing who'd turned into a wild woman one night, nearly dragging him into an empty bedroom at the end-of-semester party. The woman who'd promised sex so uninhibitedly she'd singed the edges of his imagination. The woman who never spoke up in class but who'd whispered filthy words in his ear while she'd unfastened his belt and started in on the zipper of his slacks. Unfortunately, she'd given off enough clues of her intoxicated state to keep him from following through, just barely managing to stop things before they'd gone too far.

Laura Barber . . . the one who got away. Hell, the one he'd let get away. Damn his conscience all to hell.

"Do you own this truck?" she asked after several minutes of silence.

"Rented."

"Do you always drive something so big?"

Right. The queen of green. "What were you driving?"

"A hybrid."

"If you'd had one of these, you wouldn't have gone off the road."

"Touché." She looked him in the eyes for probably the first time since she'd climbed aboard. "Truce?"

"Sure." Although, how he'd manage that would take some mental gymnastics. She wore the same scent she had all through business school. Nothing exotic, just kind of clean and sweet. She'd wrapped the scent around him that night. It still went straight to his gut, and now he had the mother of all hard-ons. Truce, indeed.

He stared out the windshield. "That your hybrid up ahead?"

She squinted, peering forward. "It is."

He pulled up beside the car, set the brake, and pushed the gear lever to park. "Leave the engine running for heat. Give me your keys."

"I can get my bag myself."

He held out his hand. "I thought we had a truce."

After fishing in her purse, she produced a key on rental company chain and handed it over. Now, he could get away from her perfume for a few seconds. Maybe the cold would do something to ease his boner too.

He climbed out of the truck and shut the door behind him. His boots sinking into snow halfway to his knees, he trudged the few feet to the hybrid and used the key to open the trunk. She traveled light—just one carry-on and a suit bag. If he looked inside, which he wouldn't, he'd no doubt find a formless skirt and jacket combination. She could almost, but not quite, hide her plush figure under all the layers of clothing she wore.

After closing the trunk, he scrambled back to the truck and stowed her things in the back. Then he took his seat in front and set the gear to low to take them down the frosted highway.

"You seem to know your way around," she said.

"I grew up near here."

"You look the part. All you need is a Stetson." She actually smiled. Not much but enough to curve that tempting lower lip. No matter how hard she tried to blend into the woodwork, that mouth and her enormous brown eyes kept her from pulling it off. Great, now he was thinking about her mouth.

"What are you doing in these parts?" he asked, even though he had a pretty good idea of the answer.

"Job interview," she answered.

"Henderson?"

"How did you know?"

"My interview is day after tomorrow," he said. "Doesn't look as if either of us is going to make it."

She groaned. "Oh no."

"Don't worry. You still have a chance."

"Why wouldn't I?" she said. "They'll understand about the storm."

"I didn't mean that. I meant the competition."

"What . . . oh." She glared at him. "You don't think I can beat you for the job."

He didn't answer but only smiled.

"Competitive to the end, eh?" she said.

"Pot . . . kettle."

"Is this your idea of a truce?"

"Sorry. Force of habit." He turned the truck off the main highway onto the narrow road that led to Jeff's cabin. Here, even the four-wheel drive wouldn't help them if he made a bad move. He'd have to concentrate on something besides the chaos in his jeans. The heavy vehicle inched along while the wipers slap-slapped against the windshield and the wind howled outside, swirling the snow around them. Laura sat huddled in the corner, her arms wrapped around her ribs.

"Frightened?" he asked.

She bit her lower lip. Even a short glimpse of that out of the corner of his eye put his mind in places where it didn't belong.

"A little," she said after a moment.

"I'll take care of you." Boy, howdy, would he. *Stop it, damn it. Now.*

Normally, she'd have bristled at any suggestion that she needed help with anything. She must have been really scared not to say a word but just sit there, making herself small. If he wasn't careful, she'd start tugging at his protective instincts. But then, when had he ever been careful where a woman was concerned? Well, maybe once . . . with this woman.

"Is it much farther?" she asked.

"A few more yards." Of course, in a storm in the mountains, a few more yards could stretch on forever. How had the pioneers ever managed?

The cabin came up on him unexpectedly. He must have misjudged how far they'd come because the outline of the building appeared directly ahead of them before he'd realized they'd arrived. He let a breath out slowly, and his shoulders relaxed. Though he'd never admit it to Laura, navigating under these conditions was a bit of a crapshoot, and he hadn't felt all that comfortable himself.

He steered the truck into the carport and cut the engine. When he turned off the headlights, they fell into darkness for a moment. All the better for him to sense the woman next to him. Her scent and the sound of her breathing filled the space around him. It was going to be an interesting few days.

If the cabin had appeared rustic from the outside, the interior somehow managed romantic and high-tech at the same time. Laura left her ruined shoes in the enclosed entryway, what Ethan referred to as a "mini mudroom," and followed him into the main living area. When he hit the switch, lights came on around the baseboards, producing enough illumination to suggest the interior of an elegant restaurant.

"Solar power?" she asked as she tipped up her carry-on and draped the suit bag over it.

"From batteries beneath the house," he said. "The system gives off heat as well as light."

"And the heat rises to fill the room."

"Once I get the woodstove and a fire going, we'll be toasty."

"Nice." They'd been bandying that word around a lot. This time, it didn't carry extra meaning.

Ethan put the bag of groceries on the counter in the kitchenette. "Settle in."

She glanced around. "Are there other rooms?"

"Bathroom."

"Then, where would you like me to settle in?"

He paused in the act of stowing a carton of eggs in the refrigerator. After a moment, he straightened, placed his elbow on the door and assumed his too-casual pose again. "You take the sleeping loft. I'll camp out on the couch."

She checked the piece of furniture in question. "Is it big enough for you?"

"I'll fold into it."

"Because, I don't really have to—"

"Take the loft. As you observed, heat rises. You'll be comfortable up there."

The baseboard heating was having an effect on the temperature, but not enough for her to remove her coat.

"I'll lay a fire," she said.

"You know how to do that?"

"It's not rocket science."

"Be my guest."

While he continued putting away groceries, she went to the huge stone fireplace and knelt to check out the supplies. Plenty of wood and kindling. Starting with crumpled newspaper, she built what should soon be a good blaze. She found matches, lit the paper, and sat back on her heels to watch the fuel catch.

Out of nowhere, a male hand appeared in front of her, holding a glass of red wine. She took it and glanced up at the towering figure of Ethan Gould. "Thanks."

"I didn't know for sure if you'd want anything to drink."

"I'm good with wine. It's tequila I need to stay away from." Damn it, why had she said that? She shouldn't have mentioned anything that could remind him of that night. Or remind herself, for that matter. She sipped some of her drink and stared into the fire.

Of course, he didn't do the easy thing and go back to the kitchenette and leave her alone with the memory. Oh no, he had to sit down beside her in front of the fire.

"Want to talk about the two-ton elephant in the room?" he asked.

"No."

"I do."

"Fine," she said. "You talk. I'll listen."

"Doesn't work that way."

"Look, Ethan." She took a fortifying sip of her wine and let it roll around on her tongue. He had good taste, she'd give him that. Eventually, she had to face him. When she did, she somehow ended up lost in the reflection of the fire in his eyes.

"Laura . . ." he prompted.

"I wasn't myself that night." Lord, how embarrassing. If he wanted to talk about this, why didn't he say something or do something? Why was he putting it all on her? "I behaved inappropriately toward you."

He gave her a lopsided smile. "Is that what they're calling it now?"

"Please. You'll make me blush."

"So what?" he said. "No one's ever died of blushing."

She could. Her heart fluttered in her chest, and her stomach felt full of cold lead. When her hands trembled, she set her glass on the hearth rather than spill red wine on the carpet.

"Hey, hey." He put his glass next to hers and took her hands in his. "It's not that serious."

When she couldn't take any more gazing into his eyes, she

switched to staring at the fire. "You could probably have sued me for harassment."

"Harassment?" he repeated. "How do you figure that?"

"You obviously didn't welcome . . . um, feel the same . . ."

"Because I didn't follow through?"

She clenched her teeth together and sat in utter, silent shame.

"You'd had too much to drink, Laura," he said. "Only a bastard takes advantage like that."

"Well," she pulled her hands from his and took a steadying breath. "It was a long time ago. I'm glad we settled it."

"I don't call that settled," he said.

She stared into the fire again. If she didn't look at him, maybe he'd go away. "I do."

"Damn it, Laura, you're going to deal with this." Taking her chin in his hand, he turned her head until she had to look at him. "Do you know how exciting you were that night?"

"I was drunk and disorderly." Drunk enough for him to have rejected her but not enough for her to have forgotten all the things she'd said to him. No one on earth had ever heard of her fantasies, but after that encounter, this man had.

"You turned me on like crazy," he said. "I went nuts trying to figure out how to get you to make the same invitation sober."

"It was a long time ago, Ethan."

"I would have called you, but I figured that would have embarrassed you."

"I'm glad you didn't."

"I kept putting myself in places where I'd bump into you

by accident, but you disappeared"—he gestured with both hands—"poof."

"I don't want to talk about this," she said. "You promised."

He studied her for a long moment before picking up his wine again. "Yeah, I guess I did."

"Thanks for understanding." This time, when she lifted her glass, it didn't wobble.

"You'll at least eat dinner with me, I hope."

"Of course," she said. "This is excellent wine, by the way."

"It should go with the steaks. How do you like yours?"

"Rare."

"Rare it is." With the knuckle of his free hand, he tapped the end of her nose before rising and sauntering back to the stove.

She took a deep breath—the first truly relaxing one she'd had since he strolled into the country store—and watched him rinse vegetables for salad in the sink. She ought to help him, but he seemed to know what he was about. Besides, the world was a safer place with distance between them.

So, he'd refused her that night out of gallantry. Or so he said. That made things marginally less humiliating. Sort of.

As he worked on their dinner, his movement fluid as he went from counter to refrigerator to cabinet and back, she couldn't erase the memory of that lean body against hers. The kisses . . . sweeter and more potent than the margaritas that had caused her to lose control. And the misery, the soul-crushing disappointment, when he'd pushed her away.

Now that they'd discussed the two-ton elephant, the whole incident was closed. Over and dealt with. Finito. Somehow, that only made her stomach sink even lower.

An Excerpt from

SOMEBODY LIKE YOU

by Candis Terry

Welcome Back to the Sugar Shack

Straitlaced . . . Chicago prosecutor Kelly Silverthorne has a perfect record in the courtroom and a big fat zero in the bedroom. When she loses her first case ever, she returns home to Deer Lick, Montana, to regain her confidence and shake off the "Sister Serious" moniker she's been strapped with since childhood. Only a few hours into her repentance, karma thrusts her face-to-face with yet another of her major fiascos—a one-night stand with the hottest cop in the county.

Rebel with a Cause . . . Deputy James Harley has always played with fire. When smart and sexy Kelly pops back into his life, he doesn't mind going for a full burn. And that might be exactly what happens when his past threatens to catch up with his future.

A Match Made in . . . Heaven only knows what Kelly's dearly departed mom has planned from the *other side*—especially since she's already meddled in Kelly's siblings' love lives. But even heaven knows that when love comes knocking, there's no stopping the good things to come.

CHAPTER ONE

Kelly Silverthorne despised killers.

Especially the type who possessed the charm of a movie star that belied the icy heart of the snake that beat in their chest.

"I think it's dead."

Jarred from the dark images in her head, Kelly looked up at her fellow Chicago prosecutor, Daniel Bluhm. A streak of sunlight shot through the window of the deli and glimmered in his golden hair. While they awaited word that the jury had reached a verdict in the Colson murder case, lunch had seemed a good idea. The nerves coiled in her stomach said otherwise. "Excuse me?"

"Your potato salad." Daniel pointed to her plate. "Or maybe I should call it lumpy soup."

Kelly glanced down at the fork in her hand and the mess she'd made of what had once been a tasty side dish. She dropped the utensil to her plate and glanced around the old-fashioned restaurant and the retro decorations that adorned the walls. "Sorry."

A smile crossed his mouth before he stuffed in the last bite of his patty melt. "Nervous?"

She nodded.

"You did a hell of a job with closing arguments."

"Daniel?" Kelly sipped her diet Pepsi and wiped her mouth with the paper napkin. "I don't know if I mentioned this or not, but this murder case we've been working on for more than a year? The case in which I pushed for an arrest and prosecution against the state attorney's better judgment? The case I swore we had enough evidence to get a conviction?"

"You mean the case that's been plastered all over the real *and* entertainment news networks?"

"Yes!" Her eyes widened in feigned surprise and she pointed at him with the straw in her soda. "*That* one. In case I forgot to tell you, it involves a popular movie-starlike senator and a glamorous cast member of "Real Housewives of Chicago." By the time I wrapped up, the jury looked at me like I'd kicked their dog."

"Don't be so hard on yourself." Her partner chuckled. "We went in prepared. We had forensics, motive, and—"

"No body." She shrugged. "Bottom line, Bluhm. No. Body." Kelly grabbed a French fry off his plate and shoved it into her mouth.

"Hey. No fair eating my food because you trashed your own."

"Partners share."

He reached across the table and covered her hand with his. "Some partners would like to share even more."

Kelly playfully poked his hand with her fork. "Not gonna happen, Romeo."

"You're killing me, Silverthorne." He leaned back in his chair. His sharp blue eyes focused on her face, much the same way they focused on a defendant he intended to break. "I've been asking you out for two years. When are you going to cut me some slack and let me take you on a date? I promise dinner, a movie, the whole shebang. I'll even be a gentleman even though it might kill me."

She laughed at the exaggerated whine in his tone. "Daniel. You are a really nice—"

"*No.*" Comically he covered his face with both hands. "Do *not* give me the *friends* speech."

His reaction sent her into a fit of laughter which helped to ease the tension churning the tuna salad sandwich in her stomach. Her phone chimed. She and Daniel looked at each other before she picked it up and checked the text message. "Jury's in."

One golden brow lifted. "Two hours to deliberate?"

Kelly nodded.

"Shit."

"Yeah." She tossed her napkin on the table and grabbed the check. "Let's go."

It took another two hours for the media to be notified and for everyone to reassemble in the courtroom. Kelly had stood outside in the warm June sunshine until the last possible moment. Praying. Searching for a lucky penny on the ground or a stray rabbit's foot. Heck, if it would mean a conviction she'd haul a whole danged bunny into the courtroom.

Her high heels clicked on the marble floor as she passed

through security, headed toward the elevator, and pressed the button. She reviewed the trial in her head while the floor numbers lit up like Christmas lights. With the exception of admitting two questionable exhibits into evidence, she'd done everything possible to nail Andrew Colson for the murder of his wife, Alicia. Over the past year Kelly had given meticulous consideration to the evidence. She'd role played. She'd spent hours and hours at the law library looking up comparable cases. She'd interviewed dozens of character witnesses. By the time she and Daniel had the case packaged and ready to present, she'd been confident they'd get a conviction.

Two hours to deliberate.

An icy chill shot up her back as the elevator doors slid open.

She wished she felt that confident now.

Inside the courtroom she set down her expandable briefcase and returned the anxious regard Daniel gave her when their gazes met. She sat down and busied herself with collecting her notes and her thoughts. Minutes later the defendant in his Armani suit and expensive haircut strolled in with his high-powered attorneys. He cast an arrogant glance toward the already seated jury then sat down and leaned back as though he were in a bar waiting for his scotch.

Geez, couldn't the guy even pretend to be human? After all, this was a trial for the murder of his wife. A woman he had pledged to honor and cherish all the days of their lives. His two children were now motherless and, if Kelly had done her job, they would be fatherless too. In a moment of sheer compassion, she felt bad about that. Not for the defendant, but for the children who would grow up forever wondering what had really happened to the woman who poured their cereal every day, taxied them to soccer practice, and tucked them into bed at night.

Kelly slid her gaze across the courtroom to where Alicia Colson's family sat together, holding hands like linked chains. They would be there for the kids. Thank God for that.

Judge Reginald Dawson entered and the courtroom stood until he was seated. Kelly gripped her pen in her hand and mentally began her customary chant.

He is guilty. He will pay. He is guilty. He will pay.

"Has the jury reached a verdict?" Judge Dawson's deep voice boomed through the packed room.

The jury foreman stood and sweat broke out on the back of Kelly's neck.

"Yes, Your Honor."

"Has the jury signed the appropriate verdict form? If so, please provide them to Deputy Southwick who will then present them to me."

As Judge Dawson opened the envelope and silently reviewed the documents, Kelly crossed her ankles and squeezed them together. Her heart pounded.

The judge passed the papers to the court clerk who then began to read. "We, the jury in the above titled action, find the defendant . . ."

CHAPTER TWO

Defendant not guilty.

They were only three words. But for Kelly they were three words that had taken all the wonderful things she believed about life and made them hideous.

Surrounded by the scent of caramel, and chocolate, and cinnamon raisin bread warm from the oven, Kelly propped her head up with one hand and shoveled another bite of chocolate chip cheesecake into her mouth with the other. When the golden retriever at her feet begged for a taste, Kelly guarded her plate like security at Fort Knox.

"Dream on, pooch."

The smooth dessert melted in her mouth while she studied the small office in which she'd sequestered herself a little over an hour ago. A calendar on the wall denoted "Sweet Sale" days at the Sugar Shack, the bakery established by her parents, now run by her kid sister, Kate. On the dinged-up desk sat a faded photo of her parent's wedding thirty-six years ago, and a photo of Kate's wedding to Deer Lick's new sheriff, taken just seven short months ago. Ceiling to floor shelves lined the back wall where a rainbow of sugar sprinkles, edible sparkles, and candy crunches lined up cap-to-cap next to an array of both PG and X-rated cake pans. Enormous differences existed between the Silverthorne women. While her mother had once created basic cakes with buttercream icing, her sister Kate's creations reflected her imaginative and often racy specialty cakes. Kelly, though she had a talent for making kickass fudge, couldn't fashion a buttercream rose to save her life.

She glanced back up to her parents' wedding photo and studied the faded print of her mother who'd died suddenly last fall. Mixed emotions rumbled around inside her heart as she thought of the last time she'd spoken to the woman who'd given her life. Well, the last time she'd heard her mother's voice. Kelly had placed her scheduled weekly call expecting their conversation would go as usual. Fluff calls, she'd come to name them because they'd become little more than generalities.

On that last call her mother had been too busy to talk. Several days later she'd returned the call but Kelly had been in court and unable to talk. It seemed like that had become the pattern of their relationship. Mom was always too busy, and when she'd find time Kelly would be unable to connect.

Kelly shoveled in another bite of cheesecake, closed her eyes, and swallowed her guilt. She'd worked in this bakery beside her family from the time she'd been old enough to hold a mixing spoon in her hand until the day she'd left for Northwestern University. Today, the place felt foreign and isolation echoed in her soul.

Her fault.

Like the inexorable loss of her mother, the events of the past month slammed through her head as if she still stood on that courtroom floor fighting for a justice that would be denied. Fighting for the rights of a woman whose life had been ripped away by a monster. A fiend now able to roam free because *she* hadn't convinced the jury of his crime.

Her fault.

She'd pushed for that arrest. Pushed for an indictment with the grand jury. Pushed for a homicide case without a corpse.

Nausea and half a mountainous slice of cheesecake roiled through her stomach as she visualized the disbelief on the faces of the victim's family when the verdict had come down. The family she'd promised that she'd get a conviction.

In her mind she could still hear the collective gasp echo across the chamber walls. She heard the grief and torment in the family's voices when they'd pointed their fingers at her and her fellow prosecutor and accused them of incompetence. Of failure.

She'd been so sure.

But she'd been wrong.

She'd never been wrong before. Never lost a case. Never led so many innocent people into such a clusterfuck of bad judgment, poor execution, and weak evidence. Not once since she'd been an intern with the state attorney's office had she ever been doubted. Until that verdict had come in. The eyes that followed her out of that courtroom and back down the hall to her office had been teeming with accusation and disappointment.

She'd failed each and every one of them.

Horribly.

She'd lost her touch. Lost her confidence. And she had no idea where to go from here.

Her sister's monstrous golden retriever pup curled around Kelly's feet and groaned as though he could read her thoughts.

"Nice try, Happy."

The pup looked up at her with big understanding brown eyes, but no one could imagine the agony and guilt that spun a toxic web around her heart. Not even the man who'd stood beside her in that courtroom for months. When the verdict came down, he'd shrugged as if it didn't matter. For him, maybe it hadn't. She'd been the one who'd had to face the family, the media, the critics. She'd been the lead on the case.

Her fault.

The office door opened and her sister with her shiny auburn hair and clashing pink apron barged into the office. The dog got up to greet her and his long furry tail swept the floor in a happy wag.

"When you said you needed to hide out, I didn't think you meant literally." Kate used her foot to scoot a chair out from the wall and she plopped down. She leaned her forearms on her knees and she studied Kelly for a good long moment. "You look like hell, big sister."

"I imagine that's an understatement." Kelly leaned back against the rickety chair in which her mother had sat to order flour and sugar for over three decades. "I haven't slept much since the verdict came in."

"You did your best, Kel."

"Did I?" The pressure between Kelly's eyes intensified.

"Yes," Kate insisted. "You used every bit of evidence you

had. Your arguments were clear and concise. You led the jury down a path where they could visualize the timeline and the crime. It's hard to win a murder case without a corpse." Kate leaned forward and wrapped her arms around Kelly's shoulders. "What more could you have done?"

"That's what I keep asking myself."

Kate gave her a squeeze then leaned back. "Well, you're home now. And if anybody in the press shows up to harass you I will personally kick their ass." Kate's brows lifted. "It wouldn't be the first time."

"It feels good to be home."

"You say that now, but wait until you're tucked into that lumpy twin bed tonight and you hear dad snoring from down the hall."

Kelly smiled for the first time in weeks. "Icing on the cake."

"Speaking of . . . I hate to impose but would you mind giving me a hand out front? I've got a few orders I need to box up and I still have to ice two dozen cupcakes for Mary Clancy's baby shower. Dad's busy with a batch of dinner rolls."

"You *don't* hate to impose, but I'd be happy to help anyway." Kelly shoveled the last bit of cheesecake into her mouth, stood, and grabbed an apron off the hook on the wall.

"Good thing you came home wearing jeans and a T-shirt instead of your usual lawyer regalia."

Kelly draped the apron over her head and nodded. She didn't think now was the right time to tell her sister she had doubts she'd ever wear another Brooks Brothers suit. Her colossal failure had led to a murderer's freedom—and there was no doubt in her mind that Andrew Colson had murdered his wife. She couldn't afford to screw up again.

Someone's life may depend on it.

She followed Kate out of the small office tying an apron around her waist and preparing herself to dive back into life in Deer Lick. She'd taken a leave of absence to attend her brother's wedding. But she'd also come home to hide. To lick her wounds. To overcome her guilt. If that was even possible. She hadn't quite planned to shovel cookies and cupcakes into white boxes, but that's exactly what she was about to do.

As she passed him in the kitchen she gave her dad a quick kiss on the cheek then headed toward the front counter. A glance over the top of the glass display case indicated a number of patrons reading the menu or pointing out sugary delights they intended to take home. Kelly's gaze skipped over the fresh Neapolitan ice cream colors of the shop, the vintage photo of her mom and dad on the Sugar Shack's opening day, and came to a sliding stop near the door. Back turned toward her, a wide set of khaki-clad shoulders blocked the summer's glare off the patrol car parked outside.

She sucked back a groan.

Apparently karma wasn't done playing *gotcha*.

Her hands stilled on the apron ties. Her heart knocked against her ribs. The knot in her stomach pulled tight. On the other side of the lunch counter stood another of her monumental screw-ups.

As if she'd called his name, he turned his sandy blonde head. His brown eyes brightened and a smile tipped the corners of lips that were sinfully delicious. She knew. She'd tasted them.

She took a wobbly step backward.

In her thirty-two years she'd been struck with accusatory

scowls from a judgmental mother and murderous glares from convicted felons, but nothing had ever hit her below the belt like a smile bursting with sexual promise from one of Deer Lick's finest.

Deputy James Harley.

His intense gaze perused her body like he was on the cruise of a lifetime and enjoying the trip. He'd looked at her that same way just a few months ago—braced above her on arms thick with muscle while the rest of his hot, hard body did the talking.

A tingle ignited from her head, sizzled like a fuse down the front of her shirt, and detonated beneath the zipper on her jeans. Her skin turned hot and a flush crept up her chest. All thanks to the memory of one night in James Harley's bed.

As a deputy sheriff he'd sworn to serve and protect. During the hours she'd spent rolling in his sheets, he'd done both. At least from what she remembered.

The night of Kate's wedding reception, Kelly knew she should have stayed focused on carrying out her maid-of-honor duties. But one too many glasses of exceptional champagne had dislodged a few of her bolts and screws and she'd completely given herself over to whim and mind-bending orgasms. Afterward, she'd made a promise to herself to get a serious handle on the sometimes uncontainable urges that never ceased to embarrass the hell out of her. Even if they did provide a real jolt of excitement.

She blinked away the sweaty memory of the hot, sexy man on the opposite side of the counter, sucked in a breath, and stepped up beside Kate. "What do you need me to do?"

"Could you box up that chocolate cake and then fill James's lunch order?"

Crap. "Sure." *Kill me now. Please.*

Her hands uncharacteristically trembled as she opened a pastry box and lifted Dr. Robinson's double chocolate birthday cake from the display case. She didn't know why her stomach was so keyed up. She'd spent the last seven years in the heat of the spotlight, prosecuting some of the dirtiest criminals in the state of Illinois, and she'd never once been nervous.

So why did taking a lunch order seem so damned intimidating?

With a smile she handed the pastry box over the counter to Dr. Robinson's nurse and rang up the bill on the register. She closed the cash drawer and wiped her hands down the front of her apron, leaving a streak of chocolate. When she looked up *hot cop* was standing at the lunch counter. Muscled arms expanded from beneath his short uniform sleeves while the fitted shirt hugged his wide chest and slim waist. Kelly knew that beneath all that khaki fabric was a talented body of pure strength and muscle. A *very* talented body.

God, her thoughts were a train wreck.

She grabbed the pencil and order pad. "Can I help you?"

A smile crinkled the corners of his brown eyes and a slow blink swept long, dark lashes across his cheeks. "You're back."

"Apparently."

He chuckled. "And you're not happy to see me."

"I'm not *not* happy to see you."

"Okay then. I'll take that for starters."

Oh, no. His days of taking from her were over. She was on a *save your soul and sanity* mission. No boys allowed. "And what would you like to eat?"

The spark in his eyes guaranteed she wouldn't need a Geiger counter to detect what he was thinking. "Sandwich, Deputy Harley. What kind would you like?"

"I'd like two tuna subs. No tomato. Two iced teas." He settled a lean hip against the counter. "And your phone number."

A laugh escaped before she could stop it. "That will be nine fifty-six."

"Is that a no?" He reached into his back pocket, withdrew a worn leather wallet, and handed her a twenty.

Her fingers curled around the money. "I'm sure you have all the numbers you can handle."

James held on to the cash, just to be able to touch her for half a second. "I'd be willing to throw all those numbers away in exchange."

Since she was a pro and could read a lie a mile away she probably thought he was bullshitting her. But he'd never been more serious.

One night with Kelly Silverthorne hadn't been nearly enough. Once she'd hightailed it out of town he'd tried to discount the hours he'd spent with her in his arms but it had been impossible. Now here she was again. And everything inside of him was buzzing with awareness.

As expected she looked up and studied his face like he'd been named a prime suspect. He knew that look. On the job he'd used it himself once or twice.

"Without all those phone numbers what would you do on a rainy day, Deputy?" Her head tilted just slightly and her ivory hair fanned like silk across her shoulder. "I'd hate to be the cause of your ultimate frustration."

"Nice jab, Counselor." James steadied his breath as he watched her delicate fingers punch the amount into the register and slide the cash into the drawer. Kelly Silverthorne was the most beautiful woman he'd ever laid eyes on. And he'd seen plenty. From the second grade he'd watched her, admired her, and had probably had a crush on her even though the only glances she'd ever returned had been rife with warnings to keep his distance.

The night she'd ended up in his bed? No one could have been more surprised. Oh, he wasn't about to complain. No way. The counselor was hot. And sweet. And way out of his league. Though he knew he'd had his one and only shot with her, he craved her like a decadent dessert or a fine wine. One taste was just not enough to satisfy.

He watched as she grabbed the sandwich rolls, cautiously sliced through them, and spread a thin layer of mayonnaise across the surface. She topped the bread with perfectly rounded scoops of tuna salad and carefully placed leaves of crunchy lettuce on top. Every movement was smooth and calculated as if she'd be judged on her placement and presentation.

In an attempt to gain control over his body and all the odd stirrings around his heart, he looked away. A quick glance at the two sisters revealed the vast differences. Kate, his best friend's new wife, was a bit taller and looked as if in a scrap she could hold her own. Her straight auburn hair displayed a meager reflection of her fiery personality. Whereas Kelly, a few inches shorter, teetered on the more delicate side. She looked like a woman a man would jump to protect. Her long ivory hair had a soft curl that made her glow like sunshine.

He smiled.

At least she'd lit up his world. For a night.

"So what made you leave the windy city and come all the way back to our little town?" he asked as she wrapped each sandwich in white paper as carefully as if she'd been swaddling a newborn.

"Just needed a break." She slid the packaged sandwich into a crisp white bag.

"Most people who need a break hit a tropical beach. Not some dusty back road to nowhere."

"Maybe *nowhere* is exactly where I want to be." She shoved the second sandwich into the bag a little less carefully.

Whoa. Was it his imagination or was he detecting some underlying aggression?

"Well, I'm sure your family will be happy to have you around for a little while," he said, watching her graceful fingers fold down the top of the bag.

She gave him no response as she set the bag on the counter, grabbed two paper cups, and began to fill them with iced tea.

"So . . . exactly how long of a little while will that be?" he asked.

The glass pitcher thunked on the counter and tea sloshed up the sides. "The length of my stay is really no concern of yours, Deputy Harley."

"True. But I'm more than willing to change that if you are."

A smile tilted her soft, full lips. "You really are incorrigible."

He mirrored her expression. "It's a cross I bear."

She set the cups of tea down in front of him and pushed plastic caps over the rims. "I hope you enjoy your lunch, Deputy Harley. Please do come again soon."

"Is that an invitation?" *Say yes, Angelface.*

Her delicate brows pulled together over sea green eyes. "Are you serious?"

"As a tortoise trying to cross the road."

"I'm sorry, Deputy—"

"I think we know each other well enough to be on a first name basis, don't you?" Her slight hesitation gave him hope.

"Like I said, I'm sorry, *Deputy*, I'm not here to engage in anything other than some rest and relaxation. I need a break. Not an opportunity to . . . lose control," she whispered.

James smiled. He knew exactly how loudly Kelly lost control. And exactly what made her lose it. Then again, he was more than willing to invent new techniques to make that happen too. Even if it took all night. *Please, God, let it take all night.*

If Princess Prosecutor imagined him as a man who gave up easily she'd be very wrong.

"You know . . ." He leaned closer and spoke low for her ears only. "If you give me your number you might just have a little fun losing a little control for the little while you're here." He lifted the bag and cups from the counter, stepped back, and gave her a good long appreciative once over. "Or is that what you're afraid of?"

An Excerpt from

A MOST NAKED SOLUTION

by Anna Randol

Lady Sophia Harding: beautiful, blonde, and . . . capable of murder? That's what Lord Camden Grey intends to find out.

Sophia knows that to keep her family's secrets she must avoid any entanglements with the powerful and brutally handsome man. But the pull of their mutual desire is all-consuming. Can Sophia trust Camden with the truth when she knows it might kill the love that grows between them?

CHAPTER ONE

Weltford, England, 1816

Sir Camden Grey glared at the ink-spotted paper in front of him. Damnation. Was that a six or an eight? Perhaps a three? He placed his quill back in the ink and pressed the heels of his hands against his bleary eyes.

He should have stopped working on the equation hours ago, but the solution had seemed so close this time. If he'd worked only a little harder or faster, perhaps he'd have been able to—

A knock again sounded on his door, reminding him of what had startled him into splashing ink everywhere in the first place.

"Yes?" He knew his tone was harsher than it should have been, but he hadn't slept in—he checked the clock—twenty hours, and his servants knew better than to disturb him. If that fool Ipswith found an answer first, Camden would never again be able to set foot in the Royal Mathematical Society. The chairman, his father, would see to it. Just as he had seen to convincing Ipswith to research the exact same theorem to put Camden in his place.

The door opened and Rafferty entered, his stoic butler façade remaining in place despite the crumpled papers littering the carpet at his feet. "There is a . . . man to see you, sir." There was a significant distaste in his pronunciation of the word *man*.

Camden raised his brow. What was he then, a goat? Really, it was no wonder he found conversing such a waste. It was an imprecise medium. "What is his business?"

"He wishes to speak to the Justice of the Peace."

Camden glanced at the clock. "At three in the morning? Has there been a death?"

Rafferty cleared his throat and didn't make eye contact. "It is three in the afternoon, sir."

Camden swiveled to stare at the drawn curtains behind him. Indeed. Amend that—he'd been awake for thirty-two hours instead of twenty. Suddenly exhaustion hit him like a blow to the side of his head. He scrubbed at the grit in his eyes. "Did he say if it was urgent?"

As impressive as the title of Justice of the Peace sounded, it usually only amounted to settling squabbles about sheep and stolen chamber pots. He wouldn't have accepted the appointment to the position at all if there had been any other men who met the requirements in Weltford save drunk-off-his-arse Stanfield.

"The fellow claims to have information on the Harding death, sir."

Camden straightened in his chair. That would be worth delaying sleep. "Where did you put him?"

"In the library, sir."

Camden stood, twisting side to side briefly to loosen the knots in his back, then strode past his butler and down the stairs.

He smelled his guest before he saw him. The air in the corridor stank of stale onions and spoiled ale. And he wasn't even in the same room yet.

Camden stepped into the library, then silently groaned when he saw his guest. "Mr. Spat?" Lloyd Spat, less than affectionately known about the village as Tubs, sat in the center of the room, his enormous girth filling the settee from arm to arm.

"Ah, Sir Camden! A pleasure to see to see you. A real pleasure." He tried to struggle to his feet but gave up after a single attempt. "There was a reward for information on the death of Lord Harding? A sizable one?"

"If your information proves to be of use." But he had offered the money over three months ago at the death of Viscount Harding. While he still found it difficult to believe the death was a result of a poacher's misplaced bullet, he found it more difficult to believe that Tubs wouldn't have come forward if he had real information. The man would do anything for his next pint. "Why wait to come forward?"

"Well, I feared for my life. Near trembled at the thought of what would happen to me if they found out I spoke."

"If who found out?" Camden focused on breathing through his mouth only.

"The men."

He was too tired for this. His only hope was a strict linear line of questioning. Camden spun the standing globe next to him absently, tapping every third line of longitude. He returned to the original question. "Why tell me now?"

"Well you might ask, sir. Mr. Haws, that greedy old bastard, has decided that my word is no longer good enough for him. He says if I'm wanting another drop of ale from his tavern, he needs to be seeing some of the coin he's owed. Now I'm rightly offended at such rudeness and I have a mind to take my business to another tavern, but my health's no longer what it was. And I need to be close to my lodgings and my dear Mrs. Spat."

So he'd decided that his next drink was worth more than information that might cost him his life. That logic would have been too much to follow on a day when fully awake; Camden stood no chance of sorting it out now.

Tubs rubbed his hands together, then glanced nervously about the room. "No one will find out the news came from me, right?"

"Not unless you tell them."

Tubs nodded, his chin disappearing into the rippling folds at his neck. "Well, then. The day after the murder I was at the tavern."

Camden had never seen him anywhere but at the tavern.

"I was sitting at my table in the corner when I heard voices behind me. It was two blokes discussing getting paid. Now I normally keep to my own business but one of the gents says, 'The deed is done?' Now I know that when men are talking about deeds, that's not something that I need to be hearing, but I was right there so I couldn't not hear them."

Camden stopped spinning the globe, his hand coming to rest somewhere in Russia. Tubs finally had his full attention.

It wasn't Camden's responsibility as Justice of the Peace to investigate crimes, only to rule on small squabbles, or for more serious matters, to decide if there was enough evidence for a criminal to be sent on to the formal court. While he gave the cases he heard his full attention, he'd never been tempted to become involved past his limited role. It was the responsibility of the victim or his family to prosecute the crime. But something about the Harding case had seemed suspicious. Camden had finally ruled with the coroner's jury because he'd had no evidence to contradict the theory of the poacher's bullet, but it had always seemed too convenient. As if someone had decided three plus three equaled five because they didn't want to be bothered to count to six.

Then the widow's powerful family had swooped in to ensure the whole matter stayed quiet. Her father and her brothers stayed at her side, keeping her distant from everyone. Lady Harding's father, the Earl of Riverton, himself, had visited Camden to ask for discretion when dealing with the case.

Camden had agreed because he knew better than to deny a powerful man like the earl without cause. He also knew the earl's oldest son, Darton, personally, and he trusted him.

To a point.

But the whole situation had made him wary. More alert. He'd asked a few questions about town but had come up empty.

Tubs cracked his knuckles, the popping interspersing his words. "Then the other fellow says, 'He fell like a sack of turnips. Easiest job I've ever done.' Then he laughed. Now I hadn't heard about the good viscount's death yet, but something in his voice made my skin fair crawl off my body."

"Did you get a good look at either of the men?"

Tubs's eyes bulged. "There's no way I was going to let them know I'd heard them. What with them being hired killers."

Camden could hear his own teeth grinding. "Then what information do you have that you think will earn you the reward?"

"Well, then they started talking about returning to London." He looked hopeful at this bit of information, then sighed when Camden didn't react. "Then one of the fellows said, 'Did you collect the rest of the blunt from her?' "

Camden stepped away from the globe. "Her?" Why had an image of Lady Harding suddenly appeared in his mind?

"That's what he said as clear as day."

"Did they give a name? Anything more specific?" Camden tried to think of what he knew of Lady Harding, but could come up with little. Oh, he could picture her clearly enough, the pretty young woman who'd lingered outside her brother's mathematics lessons when Camden had gone to tutor him almost seven years ago. The slender delicate grace of her body and the almost elfin point of her chin. He'd liked knowing that she hid in the corridor to hear his lessons.

But he knew nothing of the woman she'd become. The Hardings had been at their house in Weltford only rarely. He couldn't remember if he'd ever been invited to an event at Harding House. He'd paid little attention to the social engagements in the area. Besides, his knighthood was recent and that left him below the notice of the oldest of the blue-bloods like the Hardings.

And if he was completely honest with himself, he'd had

no desire to see the girl who'd written him the only letter he'd received while in the army—a love letter—with another man.

Tubs grunted and tugged on his ear. "No. They left right quick after that."

Camden had little reason to think Lady Harding the woman that the killers referred to. Except, why hadn't she or her family done more to find the shooter? Why had she been content with the coroner's ruling? Why had her family been so intent on keeping him away from her? They'd claimed her prostrate with grief. All his questions had gone through her father.

"Do I get the money?" Tubs asked.

"Only if your information proves to be correct." Despite his own suspicions, he had no proof that Tubs's story was true.

"But I took time away from my dear wife to come to help with your investigation."

Frowning, Camden tossed him a guinea. "For your trouble. But you get no more unless your information leads to an arrest."

The money disappeared into Tubs's pocket. "It will, sir. Everything I told you is as true as my name."

Tubs lumbered to his feet and Rafferty escorted him out.

Camden had planned to pay his respects to Lady Harding at some point, perhaps see what manner of woman she'd matured into. Now it appeared he had no choice.

She may have grown up to be a murderer.

"You want me to give away all of the books in the library?" Lady Sophia Harding's housekeeper stared at her in shock. "But, my lady, the books must be worth hundreds of pounds."

Eight hundred and sixty-three pounds, to be precise. Sophia knew. She'd purchased every one of them when they had renovated the house last year.

But now the gilded leather spines sickened her.

She took a deep breath. "Yes, every one of them."

"What will you put in here instead, my lady?" Mrs. Gilray asked.

Sophia smiled. She had absolutely no idea. She would pick what she liked. She didn't even know what that would be. Perhaps piles of penny dreadful or scandalous novels. More books on mathematics.

All she knew was that no one would have a say in it but her.

She wouldn't fret over her choices, thinking and rethinking each one. Trying to pick those Richard would approve of while knowing she'd never be able to guess correctly.

Richard was dead.

And now she intended to reclaim the library from his influence. Sophia traced a finger down the edge of one of the books. If only it was as easy to reclaim herself. "Send them to St. Wilfred's orphanage."

"Very good, my lady." Mrs. Gilray was too new to dare question her.

Sophia turned at the sound of heavy boots in the corridor. Her eyes widened at the sight of her head gardener.

Mud caked Wicken's boots and his white hair jutted out

from his head in awkward clumps. "There's an urgent matter I must discuss with you regarding the *rose gardens.*"

Sophia tried to smile as if urgent meetings about greenery were a normal occurrence, but her mind was racing. "That will be all, Mrs. Gilray."

Mrs. Gilray's fascinated gaze swung back and forth between the other two occupants of the room, but she bobbed a curtsey and glided from the library.

Wicken closed the door behind her with a click, the kindly lines on his face deep with worry. "Sorry, my lady. I know this is most unusual. But I thought it important that you know."

Sophia swallowed against sudden unease. "Is something amiss?"

"My daughter just sent word from the village. The Justice of the Peace has been asking questions about your husband's death."

"What questions?"

He rubbed his right arm, the arm her husband had broken when Wicken refused to tell Richard where she was hiding.

Sophia fought not to stare, not to choke on the guilt that burned in her chest at the stiff way the arm hung at his side.

"What enemies Harding might have had. Same as he did right after the death."

"Has anyone said anything?"

"Not as far as I know, but it's only a matter of time before one of the villagers lets something slip."

Sophia's hands clenched into fists at her sides. Sir Camden wouldn't find anything. She wouldn't allow it. Not when that slip might lead him directly to her husband's killer—her father.

Next month, don't miss these exciting e-book romances only from Avon Books!

THE WEDDING PLANNER

by Stephanie Laurens

Lady Margaret is proud to plan the town's most important nuptials—including that of a prince. But what happens when it's Lady Margaret who ultimately falls in love with the dashing Gaston Devilliers? *New York Times* bestselling author Stephanie Laurens once again wows readers with this well-crafted, steamy novella of finding love in unexpected places.

MATING SEASON: A CABIN FEVER NOVELLA

by Alice Gaines

An Avon Red Novella

What should have been a productive research trip for Gayle Richards turns into something quite different when fellow professor Nolan Hersch tags along . . . eager to prove his theory that males are naturally more sexual than females. But when Nolan tests his theory on Gayle, he just might find that failure never felt so good . . .

NINE LIVES OF AN URBAN PANTHER

by Amanda Arista

Violet Jordan has had one heck of year: Discovering she's a shifter, her best friend is a fairy, and there's a whole other world out there she never could have imagined . . . not to mention falling in love. It's enough to make the former B-horror movie script writer question her sanity. But there's no time for doubts when the fate of her city—and the world—rests on her shoulders.

LAST VAMP STANDING

by Kristin Miller

Dante doesn't know what he is: though his fangs drop when hungry and he can go without sleep, he's not a vampire . . . not exactly. What Dante thirsts for is sex and violence, not blood. Stranded in a forest with Ariana, the jaw-droppingly beautiful woman he rescued, Dante is torn between two goals: discovering his mysterious origins and protecting the woman he is quickly falling for.